WHITEHALL BABY

LAURA BARNARD

Really hope you enjoy!
Love +
Laughs
Laura Barnard
x x x

This book is dedicated to all of the wonderful women who shared their pregnancy stories with me.

1

Saturday 25th April

Charlotte

I got talked into attending this poncy evening. Eloise didn't want to come to her work function alone. That and she sold me a lie that I could persuade some influential people to let me design an outfit for them. Not that I'd ever have the guts to put myself out there like that. I really don't know why she bothered to bring me, she's ignored me most of the evening, busy talking to very important people—some best friend.

Luckily the free wine has been flowing and I've come to love our table. The funniest thing is that most of these people work for our British government as civil servants. Just goes to show, give someone enough wine and all their inhibitions disappear. I started a few silly games to break the ice and now my ribs hurt from laughing.

I throw my head back on a fresh laugh at something Ben, the guy next to me says. At least I hope it's a joke. Otherwise he's sexist. When I try to regain some composure, bringing my head down to a normal level, I catch sight of a pair of dark brown eyes watching me from the distance.

It's a total cliche to say our eyes meet across the room, but they really do, his intense stare freezing me in place. I stare back for a second, mesmerised by the extremely tall and broad man. He's gorgeous. A thick black mane of hair swept back off his face and a square angular jaw, he looks like he could bench press me with those strong arms. Yum.

My cheeks redden at my sudden dirty thoughts and I turn away in haste. How embarrassing. He doesn't want me gawking at him. I've clearly had far too much wine if I'm considering walking up to him and nibbling his chin.

Arthur

'Who's that?' I ask Gregory, spotting the most beautiful woman I've seen in a hell of a long time.

I definitely haven't seen her around Whitehall. I'd remember her shoulder length dark tousled waves, her bronzed almost luminous skin and those lips. Damn, she has the most perfect cupids bow.

The truth is that I don't see many gorgeous women in my line of work. As Cabinet Secretary, I basically work twenty-four seven. I can't remember the last time I went on a date, let alone slept with someone. Pathetic but true. But that's what happens when you're ambitious and want this country to run as smoothly as possible.

'Don't know,' Gregory responds. 'I think she came with Eloise Edwards.'

Her carefree laughter is drawing me in, melodious and almost song like. Everyone around the table is laughing with her, looking on with adoration, as if she's the most entertaining person they've ever met.

The thing attracting me to her the most is her goofiness. Here she is at The Civil Service Awards, and she's as breezy as if she were in a cafe chatting with friends. That kind of confidence is rare to find especially when it isn't coming from arrogant MPs.

She throws her head back again in amusement. When she looks back up our gazes' lock. She stares back at me, her dark eyes widening—although I'm not close enough to see her true eye colour. Her mouth gapes open and she gives me a quick once over, blushing, and then looks away.

My dick twitches just from one look. I have to meet this woman. I don't care how but I need to get her away from her mesmerised and enraptured audience of fans.

I walk up to her, shoulders straight, deciding to do it before I lose my nerve.

'Excuse me. May I have a word in private please?'

Charlotte

Why on earth does he want to talk to me? He looks so stern, no hint of a smile. Have I done something wrong? Are you not supposed to laugh at these kinds of events?

I gulp, my mouth suddenly dry. Without hesitating, I stand and follow him to the corner of the room. God I hope I'm not going to be berated publicly. Eloise would never allow me to go anywhere with her again.

I look up at him, way, way up; he must be six foot four, his presence powerful.

3

'What's up?' I ask, twiddling nervously with my necklace.

'Oh, nothing.' He smiles, exposing perfect teeth. 'I just wanted to get you away from all of those people.'

Huh? I blush crimson.

'Am I causing a disturbance?' I bite my lip.

He scoffs a laugh. 'No, I just wanted to meet you.'

'Oh.' Jesus, why would a total sex god like him want to meet little old me?

'Well, here I am,' I say waving jazz hands.

God, I hate myself sometimes. Why can't I be cool? Sure, I mean, I know I look good tonight in my homemade black backless gown with delicate chains sewn in at the neck, but still. He's in a different league.

'I'm Charlotte Bellswain.'

He smirks, as if he finds me amusing, and reaches out his hand to shake mine.

'A pleasure to meet you, Charlotte Bellswain. I'm Arthur Ellison.'

Arthur Ellison. What a strong name. It suits him. He's enormous, even bigger up close. He must have his suits specially made to fit across those huge shoulders and bulging biceps.

I nod, tucking a bit of hair behind my ear. 'Nice to meet you too.'

'Who are you here with?' he asks looking around.

'Oh, I just tagged along with my friend Eloise.'

'Eloise Edwards?' He nods with recognition.

'Do you know her?'

'Yeah.' His lips curve in a secret smirk.

What the hell does that mean? Has he slept with her or something? I must ask her. Well, if I ever see her again. She's been stuck in boring political conversation since we arrived.

'How well do you know her, exactly?' I can't help but ask.

Is it wrong to feel so irrationally jealous of my best friend possibly hooking up with this guy? *Yes, it is, Charlotte.* Surely she'd have mentioned sleeping with this sex god of a man. I'm sure he's a destroyer of vaginas.

'We work together,' he answers with a small smile.

He leaves an awkward silence between us. I hate nothing more than awkward silences.

'So...?' I rock on my heels.

Why pull me away and then leave awkward silences? Maybe he thought I was a bit of an alright from across the room, and now he's met me up close he's realised what a dork I am.

'Where do you work?' he asks, his eyes skimming lazily over my body.

I put my arm across my chest protectively, feeling exposed in my dress. Okay, so maybe he thinks I'm still good for a quick hook up.

'Oh, nothing like this. I work in fashion.'

'Fashion?' he answers with a bark of a laugh, his eyes lit up in amusement. 'Yes, that's definitely nothing like this.'

My back is up immediately. I despise being laughed at. He might as well have said I work a bimbo job. The idiot doesn't realise fashion designers created that very suit he's wearing. What a dickhead. I'm so over him.

He looks above my shoulder, as if someone has just called him and nods.

'Sorry, I have to go back to work, but it was a pleasure meeting you.'

Ah, good way to get out of it. I'm relieved. I don't have to live this humiliation anymore.

'You too,' I say, nodding with a polite smile, glad to be away from him.

By the end of the evening, the soles of my feet are on fire. I'll have blisters for days, but damn if these shoes aren't sexy as fuck. The one great thing about coming tonight was getting to dress up. You can't really dress up properly anymore. This was a glitzy event.

The infamous Alice Elizabeth Du Pont even asked me where I'd got my dress from. She's a well-known socialite married to one of the MPs. I was so proud to say that I'd designed and made it myself. She asked for my card, but I had to bullshit on the spot and say I'd run out. Yeah, right, as if I do that for a living. I gave her my number instead. After all the bumbling I did in that conversation, I'm sure to never hear from her again.

I say goodbye to the last of my table, promising to see them again at another event. I slip my shoes off, sighing in relief when my feet hit the cool floor. I look over at Eloise, just finishing off a conversation with a balding man. We're amongst the last few stragglers. Always the last to leave the party. You can take the girls out of Watford...

She shakes his hand with such intensity her strawberry blonde locks swish around her face, and then walks over to me. God I envy her sometimes. Not only is she gorgeous, all baby blue eyes and killer cheek bones, but she's got such an amazing mind. Sometimes I have no idea what she's talking about but nod along so she doesn't think I'm stupid.

'So sorry I ended up abandoning you.' She grimaces apologetically. 'And I know you wanted to leave early.'

'It's fine,' I say with a sigh. 'Believe it or not I had fun with our table.'

She grins devilishly. 'God, you want to see them in the local pub after work. Shit faced and horny.'

Eww. Most of them were in their fifties and sixties.

I bark a laugh as I collect my bag and we start to leave, weaving around the exhausted waiters collecting used glasses.

The double doors suddenly burst open and in storms Arthur, his eyes darting around. He must be searching for someone. Shame all the boring important people have left already. Then his eyes find mine again. I shiver, the same feeling as earlier catching me off guard. He has a way of looking at you and making you feel ridiculously alive. Even by accident.

He comes to stand in front of me, a big grin on his face. 'You're still here. I thought I'd have missed you.'

He was looking for me? Huh? That makes no sense.

'Nope, always the last to leave a party,' I say with an awkward smile.

He nods at Eloise. 'Can I please borrow your friend for a quick private word?'

Eloise frowns, looks to me and then him with raised eyebrows full of questions.

Dude, I have no idea what he's thinking. Is he actually mistaking me for someone else?

'Go for it,' she says, pushing me towards him.

I turn to glare at her. Why is she always so pushy?

I nearly die of shock when he takes my hand and pulls me after him urgently. I look back to Eloise with raised eyebrows as I'm tugged along after him. She shrugs and grins.

My hand feels like a child's in his giant warm one. I don't hate it.

He leads me out the doors, down a corridor and then into a big office, shutting the door behind us.

He turns, his eyes alight with mischief, pinning me

against the wall with only his dark intense stare.

'W...What's up?' I ask, my teeth almost chattering from nervous anticipation. What on earth is happening here? Guys like this don't show interest in me. Not that I've been out much in the last year.

He appears momentarily shy, his eyes finding the floor and then back to me.

'I wondered if I could take your number?' He hands over his iPhone and I stare down at it in confusion.

'My number?' I repeat like a drunk parrot. Maybe I shouldn't have had those last few glasses of wine. I can't seem to think clearly.

He grins back with a nod. Jesus, he must think I'm ridiculously stupid.

'Oh, okay.'

I quickly enter it into his phone, my fingers shaking so hard I'm sure I've missed a digit, and then hand it back to him. I just want to get the hell out of here. The guy makes me feel weirdly on edge. I don't have time for feeling like this. My life is busy enough.

'Great.' His stare drops to my lips.

I subconsciously bite my bottom lip. This guy is so unpredictable. I have no idea what's happening here. Maybe I've actually dozed off at the table after all that wine and this is just a weird dream.

He slowly stalks towards me, invading my personal space, his dark eyes predatory, until my back hits the wall with a thud. He towers over me, all strength and power. My chest heaves erratically, my breasts rising up in my dress. Is he going to kiss me?

Maybe I got knocked out at dinner? Laughed so hard I hit my head on a chair or something. I could be in a coma in a hospital bed right now.

Before I have a second to wonder he clasps his huge hands around my face and then plunges his mouth against mine. My lips set alight and move with his as my heart races in my chest.

His hands wrap into my hair, pulling harshly from the roots. I squeal from the pain, but it just makes him growl, the rumble shuddering through his chest which my hands seem to have found. A hard as steel chest, deliciously warm.

I allow his tongue to sweep into my mouth, teasing me, kissing me with thorough determination. We kiss each other like we've been doing it for years, a strange sort of comfortableness mixed with a raw sexual undercurrent. I can honestly say I've never been kissed like this.

He pulls away from me slowly and I gawk back at him, my breaths coming out in uncontrollable spurts. He grins, as if shocked with himself. Then he pulls himself together, straightens his jacket and opens the door. He grabs my hand and leads me back out to Eloise.

'Lovely to meet you, Charlotte.' He nods again at Eloise. 'Barry will organise a car for you.'

I stare back at him, still completely dazed. Did that really just happen? Or was it a fantasy in my head?

He gives me one last cheeky smile, a smile that makes him look about ten years younger, before he walks off.

'Well, what the hell happened?' Eloise asks as soon as he's out of ear shot.

'I have no bloody idea.' I touch my swollen lips, wondering if she can tell.

'You do realise who that is, right?'

'Err, he said his name is Arthur something?'

'Arthur Ellison.' She nods with raised eyebrows, like I should know him. 'He's a big deal around here. The Cabinet

Secretary. Nothing happens around here without him knowing about it.'

I shrug. Power means nothing to me, especially when it comes to politics. I'm best to just chalk it up to a wild night with far too much free wine.

2

Monday 27th April

Charlotte

*B*y Monday I've almost forgotten my random encounter with Arthur Ellison. Well, okay I might have had some bloody bizarre dreams about him. I don't know why. I mean, sure the guy is sexy as hell but he's also clearly a weirdo. Far too intense. Not my type. Nope, not at all.

I have far more important things going on in my life. Like trying to persuade my boss to look at my designs. I said I work in fashion, because I do, but I'm only a PA. I joined the company eight years ago with my fashion degree hoping that I'd quickly climb from the mailroom to being an actual designer.

Well, unfortunately, I've only ever been promoted to PA of the CEO. Despite me going for every internal interview,

I've always been refused. I've been told the problem is that
I'm too good at my job and that they don't want to lose me.
Well *sorry* for having great organisational skills.

I should really give myself a kick up the arse and leave,
but I still get a buzz even just being in the fashion
environment. Besides, what can I put on my CV? I've only
got admin experience.

Eloise has bullied me into meeting her for lunch at the
little bakery near her work. She's always saying I need to
push for a lunch break. It's so easy to get swept away in all of
the fashion drama and before you know it its 3 p.m.

So that's how I find myself sat at a small table for two by
the window. I wait on my coffee and text her to ask where
the hell she is. I hate how she's allowed to be late but
whenever I am she gets annoyed. She's been doing this since
school.

I'm just stirring sugar into my coffee when I see a huge
hulk of a man cross the street, heading for the same
cafe. Yum.

Uh-oh. My stomach wobbles as I remember those broad
shoulders. How those arms wrapped round me and held me
close while those lush lips attacked me. It's Arthur Ellison.
Shit.

I quickly look down, using my hair as a protective
curtain. Please don't let him see me. The bell above the door
rattles and I smell him immediately. God, he smells divine.
How could I have ever forgotten that smell? Like florals
mixed with citrus notes. Somehow manly, it kind of reminds
me of smelling the orange trees on holiday in Spain when I
was young.

He hasn't recognised me yet, thank God. I mean, he
might not even remember me. Maybe he kisses a different
woman each night? He could with that face.

The bell above the door dings again. I briefly look up as Eloise spots me.

'Char! Sorry I'm late, but we had a bastard getting our proposal approved.'

At Eloise's booming voice, Arthur turns his head. Our eyes meet and that same electric intensity sizzles between us.

'Oh, hi. I didn't see you there.' He takes his coffee from the barista and strides over with a confident smile.

It's actually unfair how gorgeous he is while I'm wearing a dress from Primark and miss-match underwear. Don't get me wrong, I make this plum-coloured body con dress look like its Gucci, but *I know*. Hardly the glamour puss he met Saturday night. He surveys me and it's as if he knows too.

'Hi.' I do a stupid wave. I'm such a dork.

'Eloise,' he nods curtly before thankfully leaving.

As soon as the door shuts, I let out the large breath I'm holding tight in my lungs. Jesus, that man is stressful.

'Keep it in your knickers, Char,' Eloise cackles. 'Jesus, you're as red as a tomato.'

'Great. Just great.'

I'VE JUST ABOUT RECOVERED LATER that afternoon when an unknown number starts calling my mobile. Could it be him? Nah, I'm obviously just getting excited for no reason, although I've no idea why. I want nothing to do with him. The pompous gorgeous bastard.

That doesn't stop me rushing to the toilets. I don't normally do this when I assume it's just a call asking if I've had PPI insurance.

I take a quick deep breath and press answer.

'Hello?'

My body is praying to God it's him, while my brain tells me to stop being stupid.

'Hi Charlotte, it's Arthur Ellison.' I can almost hear that amused smirk down the line.

'Oh, hi.' I'm actually out of breath. What is wrong with me? I have zero game when it comes to dating. This is why I stay away from it.

'I was wondering if you were free for dinner tonight?'

Wow, straight in there. No hesitation at all. He really wants to take little old me out to dinner? Maybe it's some kind of bet his friend made? Don't get me wrong I'm not ugly but being around fashion models all day does batter your confidence.

'Um...'

I don't have plans, but I'm also not sure if I want to jump into whatever the hell this is. Would he have given me a second thought if we hadn't have bumped into each other today?

'I don't know if I'm free,' I say vaguely, playing for time.

'Come on,' he encourages. 'You came to see me today, didn't you?'

Oh so *that's* it. He thinks I was hoping to bump into him. Thinks I'm a little bunny boiler. What an idiot. I have no time to play stupid games.

'It was a coincidence. Eloise wanted to meet there.'

'Of course she did.' Amusement laces his tone. 'We had fun together, didn't we?'

Ah, so he's just looking for a quick hook up from the woman he thinks is following him. Easy pickings for someone like him.

'I mean, for the brief time we were together, yeah... I

suppose.' I try to sound bored but it comes out uneven and jittery.

'So let me make it up to you tonight. We can get to know each other.'

He's very persuasive. No wonder he works in politics.

'Err...' I suppose I still have to eat, and God knows I have no food in at home. 'Okay then.'

It seems easier to just go with it. I've a feeling he wouldn't let me out of it if I tried.

'Yes,' he says in triumph. 'Whereabouts do you work?'

'Not far from Embankment.'

Already the thought of having to redo my make-up and engage in small talk feels emotionally draining. I was looking forward to a night of Netflix.

'Great, I'll have my PA book us a table somewhere close by and send you the details.'

God, he's a pompous dick. I *am* that overworked PA.

I already feel sick with worry, my stomach doing a million somersaults. I despise all of this awkward first date stuff. But then when I think of that kiss I find myself blushing at just the memory of his tongue in my mouth and his hands fisting my hair. Maybe it won't be so bad.

Arthur

Dammit. I was a stupid bastard to think seeing her today was some kind of sign, either from her or the universe. I just bloody knew as soon as I'd make plans they'd be some sort of emergency. It's just my luck. It's why I don't date. Too many complications when there's already enough turmoil in my life. The Prime Minister's requested an update on the budget crisis, so I've had to drop everything and rush to Number Ten.

I check my watch. 6 p.m. already. Dammit. I'll have to push the date back. I bring up her number and call her.

'Hello?' she answers, her voice quiet and unsure.

'Hi, I'm really sorry but I'm going to have to push dinner back an hour. I've been called into an urgent meeting.'

'Oh, okay. If you'd rather reschedule I really don't mind at all.'

She's not getting out of it that easily. 'No, no, I have to eat anyway. Would you be able to meet me at my apartment instead? It's closer to the office.'

'Err...okay,' she says, seeming unsure.

'Great, got to go. Bye.'

I quickly type out an email to my PA Rachel.

Please push dinner reservation back to 8pm.

Phones aren't allowed at Number Ten so I hope she replies quickly. I text Charlotte my address.

Of course, will do my PA Rachel replies.

This is why I'll never fire her. She's always at my beck and call.

I turn my phone off and leave it in the pigeonhole. I look at my wristwatch again. I can make it. Ever the optimist.

Charlotte

I've heard of some weird first impressions but this one really takes the biscuit. He rang me around six p.m. sounding completely hassled and asking if I could meet him an hour later instead. I gave him the chance to back out, explaining that I really didn't mind, but he told me no, that he had to eat anyway. What a bloody romantic.

Then he asked if I could meet him at his apartment. I just really hope it's not a ploy to get me at his house without having to take me out. Not that he seems short of cash.

I walk out of the lift and knock on his door. He's in some swanky apartment right across from the Thames. I wonder if he has a view.

Hmm, no answer. That's weird. I look to my watch; eight p.m. He told me to meet him here. I didn't have a chance to get home and changed so I'm still in my Primark plum dress with freshly applied make up.

Fucking arsehole, can't even be bothered to answer the door. I begrudgingly call him, hopping from foot to foot. Why did I even agree to this? I could be at home in my pyjamas—bra free—by now.

'Hey,' he answers, sounding more hassled than before. 'I'm so sorry, I'm still at work, it's been mental. But I have a key hidden above the door. Let yourself in and I'll be there as soon as I can.'

'Oh... um...'

'Speak soon.' He hangs up.

I can't help but feel like I've been handled. He *told* me to wait for him, didn't ask, told. I don't like being bossed around. At least not by dates.

Regardless, and feeling like an idiot, I reach for the key and let myself in. Wow, his place is stunning; floor to ceiling windows frame a perfect view of the Thames. His apartment is like a show home, all marbled floors, light grey walls and bright vibrant pictures on the wall that I'm sure cost more than my yearly salary.

I sink into his huge cream corner sofa, finding the remote control, and flick on the giant TV which must be at least a fifty-five inch. It's on Sky News and they're talking about some kind of political budget crisis. Boring.

I flick it over and then wonder if this is the political problem that he's currently dealing with. I don't even know what a Cabinet Secretary does. I pull out my phone and do a quick google search, squinting at what comes up. Well that's a long arse list that I can't be bothered reading. I shouldn't be with this guy. We couldn't be more different if we tried. I have zero interest in all that shit. Whenever I see politicians arguing on TV my automatic reaction is to turn over. This is his life.

Ah well, while I'm here I might as well make myself comfortable. I raid his fridge, starving for that dinner I was promised, and grab a bag of Maltesers. Relaxing into his squishy couch, I settle on a re-run of Friends, and decide to wait him out.

About an hour later the door opens and in he walks, sex on legs in a navy suit with matching pinstripe tie, carrying a plastic bag.

'I am so sorry,' he says with a grimace. Even from here I can tell he's had a shit day. His broad shoulders are tensed, a vein in his neck protruding, and his eyes are bleary.

'It's fine, really.' It's not, but I've been comfortable enough waiting.

He lifts the bag. 'I grabbed us a Chinese. I hope you don't mind. I just really didn't fancy sitting in a restaurant after the day I've had.'

'What happened?' I leap up, grabbing the bag eagerly from him, wondering if he has any of my favourites.

'You didn't see it on the news?' He raises his eyes up in surprise.

'I have a confession,' I admit, getting out what looks like a sweet and sour chicken. Yes, one of my faves! 'I don't really watch the news.'

His mouth drops open. 'You have to be joking.'

I sound like such a bimbo. Eloise would be so ashamed of me right now.

'No. I mean, sometimes, but if anything political comes on I turn it over straight away. I can't stand it.'

He shakes his head in disbelief. 'Jesus, and you're friends with Eloise how?'

I snort a laugh. 'People always ask me that. We've been friends since secondary school, we come from the same hometown.'

'Ah.'

'Yep.' I nod. 'I went off to do my fashion degree and she went to Oxford to study politics.'

'Yet you still remained close friends?' He frowns as if genuinely wondering how that could have happened.

'Yeah, of course. I mean, no one knows you like your school mates, right?'

He thinks about it a second as he spoons out some food to a plate. 'I suppose you're right. Although I'm not friends with anyone from school. Only university.'

I raise my eyebrows. 'Well, by the looks of it you don't have much spare time.'

He snorts a laugh. 'That's an understatement.'

We tuck into our food in silence. I hope he likes girls who eat because I am not holding back. I'm starved. I can't remember the last time I treated myself to a takeaway. As I stuff the last prawn cracker in my mouth I lean back, hoping he won't kiss me. I'd likely burp in his face.

'How did you know to get my favourites?'

He grins. 'I called Eloise. Who didn't even know we were going out.' He glances at me and arches a brow.

'Well, yeah, she doesn't live in my pocket.' I roll my eyes.

'Good to know that you're discreet,' he says, almost absentmindedly.

Discreet? Does he want to keep this all a secret?

Whatever the hell this is. I help him clear up in an awkward silence.

'Great apartment by the way.'

'Thanks.' He smiles, his eyes tired. It's only now I can see how exhausted he is; his eyelids heavy and drooping as he rubs at them. 'Just a shame I don't get to spend more time here.'

He plonks himself down on the sofa, loosening his tie and undoing his top button. It's annoying how sexy it is. I get the smallest glimpse of tanned skin. I wonder if he has hair on his chest. With dark hair like that I'd bet he does.

He holds out his arms for me, without even breaking his glance from the screen.

O... kay. He wants to cuddle? I slowly lower myself down next to him and automatically he wraps his arm around my shoulder and pulls me close, my other shoulder rests against his broad chest. Wow, he's friendly. He's acting like we've done this every night for two years, not a first date. Although I suppose you can't even call it that.

He hands the remote over to me. 'Anything but the news, right?'

I grin back at him. He's quite funny, even if it is at my expense.

I turn on a film that's already been on an hour. It seems an easy one. I allow myself to relax into his touch. The feminist in me hates to admit it, but there's something about being in a big strong man's hold that settles your nerves.

Barely ten minutes have gone by before I realise he's asleep, his light snores heard over the film. It gives me an excuse to shamelessly look over him. The glow from the TV highlights his perfect profile with its strong, square jaw. He has a small bump on his nose. I wonder if he broke it in a bar fight or something. He also has a slight bend to his ears.

You wouldn't notice it unless you were staring at him. For some reason I find it adorable. It doesn't stop him from being perfect though.

His black hair is pushed off his face and held back by gel or something. Almost like he's fresh and wet from the shower. It has a curl to it I hadn't noticed before.

I sigh. We're so different. Definitely not meant to be.

I make to get up, but he tightens his grip on me.

'Stay,' he whispers, his voice raspy.

I look over him, eyes still shut. I should really get back. I need to get the last train home.

'Please.'

I hear the desperation in his voice. It's then that it hits me. This man, although powerful and successful, is lonely. He craves human connection, just like everyone else.

'Okay.' I cuddle myself back into him, pressing my cheek into his chest and swinging my legs over his lap. I don't know how I feel about this man, but the thought of him needing me... it makes me feel useful for once. So I close my eyes and try not to think about what it means.

3

Tuesday 28th April

Charlotte

I'm woken by the clatter of cups and begrudgingly open my eyes. My neck's stiff and I crank it slightly to see Arthur sat on the coffee table in front of me. He's freshly showered by the smell of him and already dressed in another suit, this time a grey pinstripe. His taunting smirk is back on his lips.

'I made you coffee,' he says, pointing to my cup as he sips his own.

I grunt in response.

'I'm going to go out on a limb here and say you aren't a morning person.' His eyes spark with humour.

I grab the coffee and drink from it like my life depends on it. God, he's annoying, but this is damn good coffee, almost coffee shop quality.

'I'm a night owl,' I croak. 'Why would anyone like the mornings?'

He grins. 'You've got to catch the early worm and all that.' He clears his throat, his eyes quickly switching to serious. 'Well, listen, I wanted to talk to you, but now I'm thinking I should see you tonight when you're more awake.'

'Better idea,' I croak, already trying to fall back asleep when I see its only seven a.m.

I can squeeze in at least another half hour.

'Okay. I'm off then. Keep the key and let yourself in tonight.'

I've no idea why I agreed to come back. The guy is clearly just going to let me down gently. Either that or fancy a quick shag before he asks me to leave, but... well his apartment is *so* pretty. Especially when you compare his apartment to the room I rent in a house in Watford. Three other girls live there so there's a constant stream of noise and drama. Plus the guy has Sky TV. I haven't been able to watch Sky since I was at my parents. It's also just down the road from work. So convenient.

I've not been settled into the comfiest couch in the world for long, when I hear him at the door. Shit. It's only 7 p m. I thought he'd be way later than this. I scramble around, desperate to make myself appear prettier. I didn't have time to go home so just stole a hot pink sample panel dress from work. No time for lipstick so I just smooth my hair down and smile.

He hurries in, throwing his satchel down by the door.

'Hey.' He smiles.

God he's dreamy. That suit fits him like a glove.

Definitely handmade. Damn, to be his tailor. Focus, Charlotte. Focus.

'Hi.' I wave awkwardly.

He grins back like he finds my dorkiness hilarious. Glad I can be of some service.

'Would you like a wine?' He asks already going to the fridge and getting out a bottle of white.

'Ooh, yes please.' *Unless you're about to kick me out that is.*

Standing up, I walk over to the breakfast bar, accepting my drink with a shaking hand. Why does he make me so nervous? He's just a guy.

'So... you wanted to talk?' I ask, taking a larger than classy gulp. I want to get this over and done with.

He smiles, his eyes wandering down to my lips. 'Yeah... I...' He clears his throat as if he's forgotten what he's saying. 'I want to be honest with you.'

'Okay.' I nod. Another gulp of wine. He's really stringing this out.

He sighs heavily, his shoulders hunching over, hands in his pockets. 'The truth is that I'm a total workaholic. I haven't dated in years and I'm not even sure I remember how to anymore.'

I laugh. Finally something he says that I can understand. 'To be honest, I absolutely hate dating. It's all so awkward, I haven't been on one in over a year.'

He swipes his hand through his thick hair. 'Yeah, well I stupidly thought I'd be able to, but yesterday just proved to me that I can't. You see, I'll always choose work over you, over anyone. My job is important and I'll just end up letting you down.'

Just as I thought; the 'kind let down'. At least he's choosing to be nice about it. He could have just never called me again.

'That's totally fine,' I say, sounding more chilled than I feel as I toe my boots back on.

He stands in front of me. 'But…'

I look up at him, his expression pensive. My chest is heaving all of a sudden, the room unbearably hot. His dark brown eyes draw me in, hypnotising me. I need to leave. Need to get out of here before I do something stupid, like stand on my tippy toes and kiss him.

'But…' he continues, swallowing hard, his Adam's apple bobbing up and down. 'There is just something about you.' He tucks some of my wayward hair behind my ear.

God, if anyone else said this shit to me I'd laugh in their face. It's such an obvious line. He's telling me he doesn't want me but fancies a quick bunk up before I go.

If I had any self-respect I'd tell him to get lost. Only it turns out I don't. It turns out he's too good looking to think properly in front of.

One night with a sexual god like him would keep my bedtime fantasies going for months. Allowing myself to feel wanted, sexy even, well it can't be a bad thing. Can it? And when was the last time I did something truly crazy without thinking it through?

I press up onto my toes before I can reason with myself. I hover close to his lips, so close his minty breath is mingling with mine, while I look into his eyes wondering if he wants this half as much as I do. He's warring with himself, just like I've been.

'Fuck it,' he growls.

He slams his lips down onto mine. I almost fall back from the force, but he steadies me by putting his gigantic hands through my hair, fisting to the point of pain.

4

Four Weeks Later - Friday 29th May

Charlotte

I've checked and re-checked but the results are right in front of me. My period isn't just being fashionably late. That amazing night of raw powerful sex, of letting myself be controlled by that beast of a man... well it's resulted in a positive pregnancy test. I don't even want to think of the word baby yet. Not until I've decided what to do.

I mean, shit. Only I could get pregnant from a one-night stand. Plus, I'm sure we used condoms. Maybe one split? God, or maybe I'm just the unlucky person who is that 0.01% unlucky.

I look around at the dingy bathroom in this house I share with three other women. There's definitely damp growing by the window. The landlord keeps telling me it's just condensation from the crappy windows, but I know better. I can't have a baby in this madhouse.

I'll have to move home to either Mum or Dad's—doesn't matter who I choose the other one will still be pissed off and complain. Divorced parents that hate each other sucks, plus the fact that both of them live miles away in Devon.

What will I do for money once I move there? I suppose I could survive on maternity leave for a while but then I'd have to return to work. It's not like Devon is well known for its fashion houses. I'll have to get some boring regular job that I hate. That's if I can even land one.

Maybe I'll be better off claiming benefits. God, just the thought of scrimping by fills me with horror.

I have no idea what I'm going to do. Each and every option sounds impossible. Maybe I should consider an abortion. It's just... well, something deep within me already knows that I wouldn't be able to go through with it. I'm all for every woman's choice, but now that it's *my* choice I don't think I can.

For now I'm just going to ignore it. Bury my head in the sand and pretend this isn't happening. I have time to decide. Plenty of time.

Two Months Later - Monday 27th July

Arthur

I know it's stupid but I still think of her occasionally. What can I say? It was a night to remember. While she was awkward, with her little waves and offbeat vibe, she was a firecracker in bed. Pawing greedily at my clothes, letting me take her over the breakfast bar, against the wall... in the bed.

Damn it was hot. Her body was phenomenal, her skin as soft as silk.

Maybe I just think its hotter because I know it was only one night with no strings. I didn't have the pressure of a future to hold me back.

Eloise passes me in the corridor.

'Eloise!' I call after her, far too eager. *Way to play it cool, Arthur.* 'Have you heard from Charlotte?'

She frowns. 'My best friend? Of course I've heard from her. Why?'

I'm not sure if Charlotte would have told her about us. She knows we had that one date, but more than that I don't know.

'Just wondered how she was keeping.'

'Yeah, she's good.' More frowning. 'She's actually got a job interview here today.'

A stone drops in my stomach. Here? She wants to work here?

'Really? What department?'

'PA to Roger Fielding.'

This makes no sense. I scrunch my face as I process it through.

'I thought she worked in fashion?'

She sighs. 'She did but they never actually let her have the job she wanted. I've been telling her forever to leave.'

'So what made her change her mind?'

Dammit, the woman intrigues me.

She bites her bottom lip. 'Erm... a change in circumstances, you could say. She's realised she has to get serious.'

My heart hammers inside my chest while my head tries to tell itself that she probably hasn't given me a second thought. Gorgeous women like that aren't short of men wanting to wine and dine them.

'What time is the interview? I might pop over and wish her luck.'

She rolls her eyes. 'She doesn't need distracting. She's nervous enough as it is.'

The thought of her awkward, all nervous and twitchy, does strange things to my dick.

'Okay.'

I'm already emailing my PA to find out the time and meeting room.

Charlotte

'So you speak French and Spanish. Any other languages?' the short tubby man in his early fifties asks.

Oh damn, I knew they'd need more languages. He's the Permanent Secretary of the Foreign Office for Christ's sakes. I should never have applied for this job. He's gonna laugh me out of the room. Especially when he finds out I can only ask where the nearest hostel is in each language.

'And I see you have a degree in fashion.' He looks down his nose at me, his spectacles on a string falling down. 'Tell me how you think that could help you in this job.'

'Err... well,' I gulp, 'despite doing a fashion degree and originally wanting to be a designer, I fell into a PA position at a fashion house. It's that role has given me the skills to do this job.'

He frowns, unconvinced. 'It's a very fast paced environment. Very stressful. Do you think you'd be able to manage that?'

I smile confidently. 'I've survived the last eight years in an industry known for being cut throat, and during fashion week, well, I'm sure it doesn't mean a lot to you, but it's as stressful as you can get.'

He chews on his lips thoughtfully.

'I'm good at meeting deadlines, communicating and getting stuck in. Yes, I might not have experience in the Public sector, but at least you know this isn't a steppingstone for me. I want a steady job for the next ten years.'

Lies. All lies.

He rubs his chin thoughtfully. 'Hmm. I've seen a few candidates that I know would want to leave within the year.'

I don't tell him that I'll also be leaving. To have a bloody baby. I still shudder at the very idea.

Eloise told me to just shut up and act surprised if and when I get the job. I found out the maternity package at my current job is basically statutory. Not enough for us to survive, even with moving back in with Mum or Dad. This job has a great package and even better salary which means I'll be able to save a bit each month. God knows baby stuff looks expensive.

A knock on the door startles us both. A head pokes through the door, quickly followed by a huge body. Oh my God. It's him. It's Arthur.

Eloise told me I shouldn't bump into him here. Not that I've told her he's the father. She just thinks that we had a Chinese that night, that he said he was too busy for dating and I went on home. I've had to bullshit and say I had a random one-night stand with a designer from work.

He smiles at both of us, as if unshocked to see me. Shit, maybe he's completely forgotten me already. Maybe he lied and I'm on a long list of women he beds. The shame settles on my soul that I could be just another notch on his bed post.

'Roger,' he says cheerily. 'I just wanted to come in and tell you what a fantastic candidate Charlotte is.'

He did? What the hell? He remembers me *and* he's trying to help me get a job? Why?

'Oh really?' Roger says with an amused grin, looking between us both.

'Oh yes.' He perches himself on the edge of his desk, his dick ridiculously close to my face. Jesus. Do *not* look at it, Charlotte. Do not think of all the delicious things he did to you with it.

'I've heard excellent things from her previous employer.'

What a total lie. Why is he trying to help me? What's in it for him?

'Jolly good,' Roger says with a nod. He looks back to me. 'I'll be in touch soon.'

Ah, he's dismissing me. Wants to talk to Arthur in private. Probably to tell some sexist man joke about me.

I quickly stand, careful not to stick out my stomach. Not that I'm showing at all yet, but I'm still self-conscious about it. Especially with the father of the baby in front of me.

'Thank you for the opportunity.' I turn to leave.

'I'll show you out,' Arthur says, following me and guiding me out of the room by the small of my back. Just that touch has my body igniting. Damn hormones.

He guides me into the long hallway. As soon as we're out of ear shot he turns to me, his dark brown eyes shining bright. I can smell his floral and citrus aftershave and its doing things to me.

'Well, this is a wonderful surprise.'

I snort. 'You didn't sound so surprised back there.'

'Well I bumped into Eloise. She told me.' He narrows his eyes at me. 'I thought you were a fashion designer.'

'I said I *worked* in fashion,' I correct him. 'I didn't say doing what.'

He looks shocked and impressed. 'I suppose you're right.'

'I am.'

God, just looking at him, the father of my baby, makes me want to smash him over the head. Stupid strong sperm bastard.

He quirks one eyebrow up. 'Well, maybe we should celebrate?'

I stare up at him. People pass us in the hallway. I lower my voice to a whisper, trying desperately to control my growing anger.

'Sorry, but are you seriously asking me to consider a celebratory shag?'

His mouth falls open, his eyes bulge. 'Err... I was going to suggest going for a drink.'

'Oh.' Well now I look crazy. 'Well, I'm afraid the answer is still no.'

God, I miss alcohol.

He turns his head to one side, his brow furrowed. 'Really? Why not?'

He's obviously never been turned down before.

I search around for an answer that doesn't include me screaming *because you ruined my life and I never want to see your gorgeous face ever again.*

'Because you're a workaholic. And so am I. That means neither of us will have time for the other. So best to just nip that in the bud.'

I storm off, eager to put as much space between us as possible, but he runs after me.

'Are you upset because I didn't call you...' he lowers his voice to a whisper, 'You know, after?'

I gasp. 'No.' I'm insulted that he thinks I'm some clingy bitch that didn't listen to his whole speech.

'Then what is it?'

Gorgeous bastard can't understand why I wouldn't want to go out with him.

I sigh, quickly counting to ten in my head.

'I just don't have the time. I'd kindly ask that you leave me alone if I get the job here. Which to be honest, is doubtful.'

I turn and stride away and don't look back until I'm near the tube.

Arthur

What the hell crawled up her arse? She's like a completely different person to the one I met a few weeks back. Where's the carefree cute woman I had screaming with ecstasy in my ear? Now she seems so serious.

It's sad that I realise I admired that she wasn't obsessed with her job like me. I suppose selfishly I want to find someone willing to fully give themselves over to me. To really care for me. Hell knows I need it. The hours I work are killing me, sometimes at the end of the day I want nothing more than just a warm body to press against. Someone to hold me. Dear God, not sleeping has turned me into a pussy.

If I went to a therapist they'd probably say it stems back to being sent off to boarding school from the age of eight. Not having a motherly touch helping to raise me. Whatever, I've done very bloody well without my parents smothering me.

Doesn't stop me feeling drawn towards Charlotte though. It's not just the thought of having red hot sex again, it's having someone to talk to without it turning political. Maybe I *am* ready for a relationship. I just need to find someone available at my beck and call. Someone willing to take second place to this job. *Yeah, good luck there, Arthur.*

I walk back into Roger's office unannounced.

'So, what do you think of Charlotte?'

5

Monday 17th August

Charlotte – 18 Weeks Pregnant

I don't know how I managed it but I'm starting work at Whitehall. I have my twenty-week scan in two weeks' time so I need to get my feet firmly under the desk before I drop that bombshell on my new boss.

Luckily for me I've had little morning sickness and I'm finally starting to feel more energetic. If I hadn't have had my twelve-week scan and seen the baby with my own eyes, I'd be assuring myself I wasn't really pregnant.

I finally told Mum, who took it far better than expected. Said she was glad I wasn't leaving it too late to have a child. I'm thirty-one, hardly a geriatric pregnancy! She also said she was glad I was doing it alone. That's right, my mum was pleased I'm going to be a single mother.

'At least you won't have to rely on a man. You can do everything your way. God, the amount of times your father would pipe up and tell me I was doing something wrong. That on top of a crying baby is just hell, sweetheart.'

Any excuse to remind me that I was a demonic baby that cried twenty-four hours a day and throw in an insult to my dad. I just hope the demonic baby gene doesn't get passed down. Mum didn't offer for me to come and live with her, but I'm assuming she'll have me.

Dad however took it differently. Makes me wonder how the two of them ever got together. He was silent on the phone for a solid two minutes. Then he got me to go through all of my finances with him and insisted I'd have to move in with him when the baby was born. I've said I'll have a think about it.

I just hope I don't see Arthur while I'm here. Eloise keeps pressurising me into telling her who the father is; she wants an actual name. No doubt so she can hunt him down and kick him in the balls.

I know she's right. Arthur does have a right to know. Well, some days I think that, but then on other days I think, *fuck him*. He quite happily had no strings attached sex and didn't bother to check if I was alive after it. I could have been hit by a bus the next day and he'd never have known.

The worst thing is the fear that he spun me a lie and does this a lot. Meets woman, draws them in and then plays that whole *'I can't commit'* thing on them before releasing his devilish hypnotic eyes and bedding them immediately.

In a way it would be all too easy to ignore him and not tell him. Hope he doesn't work out the dates, and if he does, tell him he's got it wrong. What kind of right does he have to this baby anyway? He hasn't made us any promises. Hasn't made any commitment to me.

Ugh, but I know it's the right thing to do. Damn me for being raised right. My parents might be mental but they got something right. I *will* tell him. Eventually. When I learn a bit more about him.

Arthur

I haven't slept the few little hours I normally would for the last couple of weeks. Not since I saw Charlotte again and not since she blew me off with total disregard. But today is the day. She's starting here thanks to some pretty heavy-handed persuasion on my part.

And I've decided; she's mine.

I'm claiming her. Before any of these swarmy bastards get a good look at her, I'm making her mine. I don't care what I said and what I know. I want her back in my bed and unavailable for anyone else. Sure I can't offer her what she wants, but I'm a selfish bastard. If I can't have her, no-one else can either.

I stop in front of her desk holding out a coffee.

'Happy first day.' I attempt my most charming smile.

She rolls her eyes and begrudgingly takes it from my hand but doesn't sip from it. Well this is awkward. I rock on my heels, trying not to gawk at her arse in that baby blue pencil skirt. She's going to stand out here just from her love of colour.

'From what I remember you loved your coffee. Couldn't slurp it down quick enough.'

She glares back at me. 'Yeah, well a lot has changed.'

I grimace. This couldn't be going worse.

'But thank you,' she says quickly, obviously remembering her manners no matter how pissed off with me she is.

'Well, I just wanted to wish you luck.'

She looks up at me and not for the first time I'm blown away by her natural beauty. It must be because I haven't seen her in a while, but she actually looks better than I remember. Her shoulder length brown hair seems thicker, her skin more luminous. Even her breasts look bigger. Man have I got it bad.

'You've said it. Thanks.'

And that's me dismissed.

Tuesday 1st September

Charlotte – 20 Weeks Pregnant

Well, I hate to admit it but after working here for two weeks I'm starting to understand Arthur. I don't stop from the minute I get in, until I leave. I see him now and again, always walking in such a hurried pace that he might as well be doing a light jog. He exudes such an authority, I see people scuttle around to help him pass by. It's sexy as fuck.

No wonder he was honest about not having time for a relationship. I barely have the energy to make myself dinner by the time I get in every night. I'm throwing on any old clothes in the morning, too tired to care, which is so unlike me.

I've found myself breaking down in tears on the phone to Mum or Eloise about it. I swear it's not the hormones, it's just pure exhaustion. Who knew growing a human being would be this tiring?

It's my twenty-week scan today, and Eloise is coming with me. In my head I was expecting myself to have told Arthur by now. Given him the chance of coming with me, but I've barely seen him. I suppose I wasn't exactly friendly when he offered an olive branch. I doubt he'd have the time to come with me anyway.

Eloise smiles back at me as the sonographer places the wand over my jellied belly. I still haven't got much of a bump, but that just has me worrying more that they're going to find something wrong with the baby. Maybe it's not growing properly.

Its image is reflected on the screen, far clearer than the last scan. Its heartbeat plays strong. Thank God. The cheery middle-aged sonographer does some measurements.

'All is looking good and we are expecting a due date of 19th January.'

Eloise smiles wide, her eyes glassy. 'Can we have two sets of photos please? One for her and one for the daddy.'

She smiles. 'Of course. Many fathers can't make it to the scan.'

Eloise looks at me with raised eyebrows. I know what she's saying with her eyes. *You need to tell the daddy,* and more importantly *you need to tell me.*

I wipe the jelly off, rush to the toilet to relieve my bulging bladder and then back to Eloise's judgemental eyes.

'It's just very complicated,' I say for the millionth time.

'Yeah, yeah.' She dismisses me with a wave. 'That's why you have me as a sounding board. There's nothing too complicated that I can't solve. I work for the government for God's sakes.'

I snort a laugh. 'Trust me, it's because you work for the government that I don't want to tell you. It affects you too.'

'What? What the hell are you talking about?' She stops and turns to face me in the corridor, eyebrows raised. 'Tell me, Char. Who is it?'

I lean against the wall, my legs tired. No, scratch that, my whole body is tired. I just want to face plant a bed and hide under the covers for the next year.

'It's Arthur. Arthur Ellison.'

6
_____

Arthur

*W*ork has been crazy this last week. Oh who am I kidding? Work is always crazy, but it's been especially so. I've tried to get Charlotte out of my head, but she keeps invading my mind. Every time I see someone gulping down their coffee like it's a lifeline. Every time I see a packet of Maltesers in the shops.

I'm just on my way to a meeting when I see Eloise up ahead, her strawberry blonde hair swishing around her bum.

'Eloise!' I call after her.

She spots me, eyes widening and tries to run. What the hell? I don't have any outstanding projects due from her department, so I've no idea why she looks so worried. I run to catch up with her.

'Eloise,' I say, touching her arm. 'Did you not hear me calling you?'

'Err, no.' She crosses her arms against her chest,

avoiding eye contact. Why is she so pissed? I haven't blocked anything she's tried to pass lately, she must just be on the rag. 'What is it you need?'

'I was just wondering how Charlotte was getting on?'

She scoffs and rolls her eyes. 'Why don't you bloody ask her?'

'Well,' I put my hands in my pockets, 'I got the impression that she didn't want me near her.'

'Do you blame her?' she says under her breath, just loud enough for me to catch.

Why are they so angry with me?

'What did you say?'

'Nothing. Just... ugh, go talk to her.' She spins on her heel and storms away.

Jesus, women. I'll never understand them.

Wednesday 2nd September

Charlotte

I've barely settled back at my desk after being lumped with a mountain of work from Roger, my heartbeat starting to return to a normal rhythm, when Arthur appears in front of me. Damn, does he get sexier every time I see him? He's just got such a strong presence. I can sense him before I see him.

'Hi.' He smiles, scratching his neck.

Do I detect nervousness?

'How are you settling in?'

I sigh but nod. 'I'm okay.' I try to smile, but I'm so exhausted my lips don't really work right now.

He frowns, tilting his head to one side, his dark eyes surveying me.

'Really? Because you look like you're exhausted.'

Just what you need. Someone telling you that you look like shit.

'Gee thanks.' I roll my eyes and try to busy myself by shuffling some papers.

'Why don't you let me take you out for lunch? Cheer you up a bit?'

I stare up at him. He looks so hopeful. 'I thought you don't have time to date?'

Shit, that sounds like I want him.

'I never said it was a date,' he corrects with that annoying smug smile. 'Just a lunch between friends.'

'Really?' I even sound exhausted.

His eyes make him look like the devil, offering me a poisoned apple that I just can't resist taking. I now have much more sympathy for that Eve woman.

Saying that, this could be good. I could ask him loads of questions, get to know him a bit better.

'Okay.'

He blinks, clearly shocked I've relented so quickly.

'Great.' He beams back at me like I've just made his day. It warms my heart. 'I'll come and get you at one.'

Arthur

I can't actually believe she agreed to lunch with me so easily. I was expecting a harder fight.

She insisted on eating at Pizza Express, even though I said we could go anywhere. I understand when she's wolfing down the dough balls. Damn, she likes to eat. It's so refreshing. Most of the women I know stick to salads.

'So,' she says around a mouthful of dough. 'Where did you grow up?'

God I hate all of these small talk questions.

'London, but I was off at boarding school in the country most of the time.'

'Did you like it there?' she asks, her eyes thoughtful, as if genuinely interested.

A clear memory of me being around eight years old and crying because I didn't want to leave my mum pops into my mind. I don't want to slag them off though, I know I'm extremely privileged.

'I mean, it did me a lot of good. Made me independent, gave me a great education.'

She grins, raising her eyebrows. 'That isn't what I asked.'

She's good at calling me out.

She dunks another dough ball in the butter. 'Put it this way, if you had a kid of your own, would you want to send them there?'

The idea horrifies me.

'God, no.' I steal a dough ball from her plate, ignoring her death glare. 'Not that I plan on having children.'

Her mouth drops open. 'What, like *ever*?'

I shrug. 'I mean, potentially one day. In like ten, fifteen years maybe. I just don't have the time to be a father.'

She looks crestfallen. Does she want a baby in the next few years or something? She doesn't strike me as a baby mad woman, not that I spent much time getting to know her before ripping her clothes off.

She chews, looking down at the table as if lost in thought. 'Are you close with your parents?'

I shrug. 'Not really. What about you?'

She smiles and it brightens my heart in an instant. It scares me how already her happiness is tied to my own.

'Yes. Well, not like crazy close or anything, but we get on well. They divorced when I was eleven, so they've always been more bothered about scoring points against the other to worry about me. So I could never really rebel.' She snorts a laugh. 'They're actually quite cross I've gone into civil service work.'

I gawk back at her. Surely a secure career like that is every parents' dream? Not a frilly job in fashion.

'God, why?'

She smiles fondly. 'They want me to follow my dreams and become a fashion designer.'

I nod. 'Bit unrealistic though, isn't it?' Her face drops, as if I've just kicked a kitten. 'I just mean in this current climate,' I quickly add, not wanting to sound like an arsehole.

She rolls her eyes. 'God, you're so rigid. Haven't you ever had a dream?'

So she's a day dreamer.

'Yes.' I nod. 'I wanted to change this country for the better. The way I see it, the job I do is making a difference. Sure, the general public moan about whatever we do, but I try my best every day to make England a better place to live. I won't stop until it's the best country in the world.'

She smiles up at me, her eyes filled with affection. 'You're cute.'

I frown back at her. 'Excuse me?' I have *never* been called cute. Not even by my mother when I was a boy.

She grins and shrugs. 'I said you're cute.'

'I have never, in my life, been referred to as cute.'

'Well, there's a first time for everything.' She sticks her tongue out at me.

I can't remember the last time someone stuck out their tongue at me. Actually yes I can. It was in primary school. She is beyond ridiculous. But, well... she's very sweet and endearing.

'Are you close with your grandparents?' she asks out of nowhere.

'Err... no, they've passed away.'

She chews on her bottom lip. 'Oh really? What age did they pass away? And what from?'

Well she's bloody nosy. She's going to ask me what I earn next.

I shrug. 'I don't know about three of them. They passed before I was even born.'

She chews on the inside of her cheek as if this means something to her.

'I was close to my paternal grandmother. She died when I was sixteen.'

She smiles as if this bit of information makes her happy.

'And what did she die of?' she asks, leaning forward for my reply.

What on earth is going on here?

'Heart attack.' I clear my throat, eager to change the subject. 'Anyway, how is the job going? Why do you seem so exhausted?'

She sighs. 'It's just the long hours and the commute home. It's too much for me sometimes.'

'Where do you live?'

'Watford.'

'Jesus! How long is your commute?'

She shrugs. 'Door to door about an hour and a half. Not bad really.'

God, if I lived there I'd just be travelling home to sleep and back again. At least I'm lucky enough to live nearby.

'Well, if you're ever working late and tired, you're more than welcome to crash at mine.' She looks up at me quizzically. 'As friends of course,' I add.

She smiles sadly, shaking her head. 'That's really generous of you, but I wouldn't impose.'

I laugh. 'I've told you how much I'm home. My flat just sits there empty most of the time. It would be nice for someone to use it.'

'Still.' She fidgets, biting her lip. It makes me remember when she bit mine, just the memory has my dick twitching. 'I'm just a stranger to you.'

I grin at her as memories of her naked flash through my head. Those pert breasts, peachy bottom.

'You're far more than a stranger to me.'

We stare back at each other with secret smiles. I think it's possible she's remembering us naked too. From the screams I know she enjoyed herself.

'Besides, you've been there alone before and I didn't notice anything missing.' I try to hide my grin.

'Charming!' She pouts but her eyes crinkle.

I take the key off my keyring. 'Here, take the key. I'll use the spare.'

She frowns at me, shifting uncomfortably in her seat. 'You're serious about this?'

'Yes.'

She chews on her lip again. 'And you do understand that this doesn't mean you can sleep with me?'

I bark a laugh. 'Jesus, Charlotte. What kind of arsehole do you take me for?'

She straightens her shoulders. 'I just want to be clear from the beginning.'

'Well, that's understood. I'm just trying to be a nice human here.'

'Not used to it, are you?' She laughs. 'Don't worry I'm only joking. I really appreciate it. Thanks.'

But something deep within me tells me she'll never take

me up on my offer. She's too damn proud. She's going to be a tough nut to crack.

Thursday 3rd September

Charlotte

I really wish he hadn't been so charming. It must be the baby hormones, but I found myself lusting over him when I should have just been digging for information. Both sets of his grandparents being dead worries me. What if it's from a hereditary disease that I'm now passing onto my baby? Surely I should know about that.

Roger has had me working non-stop all day. Thankfully Eloise dropped a sandwich off to me. I'm bone crushingly tired by the time I log off my computer at seven p.m.

God, the idea of commuting home on the sweaty trains just to get home and pass out in bed exhausts me even more. I could always take Arthur up on his offer. Crash at his. What if he's home though?

Well maybe I'll walk there and if it's empty I'll have a quick nap. Give myself the energy to travel home. Yes, that's what I'll do. I'll be gone before he's back. He'll never know.

I let myself in, calling out for him. Thankfully he's not back yet. Knowing him he could be gone for hours yet. I open up the fridge needing to eat something. There's another pack of Malteser's in here with a post it on it that says, *Charlotte*. Shit, he knew I'd come. I hate being predictable. Still, its sweet he remembers I like them.

I take the bag, regardless, and demolish them within minutes. I rest my head back against his ridiculously comfortable sofa and feel my eyelids grow heavy. I should set an alarm for an hour's time, but I've had such broken sleep lately, what with me constantly peeing. I'm sure I'll wake myself up. And right now if someone offered me a million pounds to raise just my pinkie I'd still ignore them.

I breathe in Arthur's aftershave, the citrus notes bringing me back to Spain, the thought of the crashing waves soothing me further. It helps drift me off to the land of nod.

Arthur

I'm quite upset that Charlotte hasn't taken me up on my offer. I keep stealing glances around work and she looks so tired, permanent purple bags under her eyes. I'm not sure she's cut out for this job and these mad hours, but I'm quickly realising she's stubborn.

I put the key in the door at nine p.m., dropping my satchel to the floor. When I find she's curled up asleep on the sofa, I freeze, my mouth falling open. Relief blooms in my chest. She came.

I tiptoe over, taking my chance to look at her unashamedly.

God, she's beautiful. A natural beauty that you don't see much of these days. Her dark lashes are such a contrast against her perfect olive skin. Her lips are parted ever so slightly, the tiniest little snore coming from her perfect cupid bow lips.

I can't let her sleep out here. She'll wake up with a cricked neck. Before I attempt to reason with myself, I scoop my arms under her neck and knees and walk her to my bedroom. She smells amazing, like sweet flowers. I can imagine the advertising hook for the perfume she wears is something about 'a whirlwind of happiness and fantasy.' *So Charlotte*. Head in the clouds daydreamer that she is.

I pull the covers back and place her in my bed. Damn, she looks good in here. I could get used to the view if she'd be willing to attempt a shit relationship with me. A workaholic with commitment issues.

I strip off to my boxers, grabbing a t-shirt from my drawers, and slipping it over my head. I crawl into bed with her, careful not to touch. Only, I'm such a big bastard the bed ends up dipping. She stirs, moaning out. I freeze, listening to her groan.

She turns to face me, eyes still shut and then snuggles right into my chest. The heat of her is so soothing. So soothing that I can't stop myself from wrapping my arms around her, letting the sound of her relaxed breath drift me off to sleep.

7

Friday 4th September

Charlotte

I wake up feeling unbearably hot. It takes a second for me to realise that I'm stuffed against a chest. Oh no. I look up and see Arthur asleep and that I'm in his bedroom. What the hell?

I feel around under the covers, relieved to find I'm fully dressed. God, did I sleepwalk into bed with him? I must have. Or he found me asleep on the sofa and he carried me in here? I smile, my heart soaring. See things like this make me believe he's a good person. That he could be a good dad. And I know it's ridiculous, but a tiny glimmer of hope that he might like me for more than a quick shag blooms in my heart. Or maybe I'm getting confused with a hungry belly.

I creep out of bed and tip toe to the kitchen. It takes me a while to figure out his fancy coffee machine, but I finally get it working while I stuff a croissant in my mouth. I always wake up ravenous these days, plus the fact all I had for dinner was a packet of Maltesers. Mmm, it's so buttery soft. I can feel it going straight to my thighs.

I turn round to find Arthur leaning against the bedroom doorframe, grinning, dressed in only boxers and a t-shirt. My god his calves are glorious. Muscly with the faintest smattering of dark hair.

I must look a mess, a whole croissant hanging from my mouth, my hair like a bird's nest. I haven't even checked to see if I have sleep in my eyes.

'Good morning,' he says, lips hooking into a smirk. His hair is ruffled with its natural curl. It makes him look younger, more carefree.

Will our baby have curly hair? I imagine a little boy like him, big brown eyes and curls. My ovaries quiver. *Yeah, yeah, we're already pregnant.*

'Err, hi.' I pick the croissant out of my mouth. 'Sorry to just help myself. I woke up starving.'

'It's fine,' he says with a dismissive wave. 'My housekeeper keeps buying them even though I tell her I don't eat breakfast.'

'You don't eat breakfast?' I repeat in horror.

What kind of a freak am I having a baby with?

He shrugs. 'They normally feed us a breakfast buffet in the morning meeting at work around eleven.'

By eleven I've had toast, a crumpet, kit kat and a pastry.

I take the mug of coffee I've made and give it to him, starting another one for myself.

'Thanks.'

'So, what happened last night? Was I just passed out and dribbling when you came in?'

He laughs, his eyes kind. 'You weren't dribbling, but yeah. To be honest, I didn't think you were going to take me up on my offer.'

'Honestly, neither did I. But I was just so exhausted last night. The thought of the commute almost had me in tears.'

I do feel well rested. Although I have no idea how I'll rock up at work wearing the same outfit as yesterday. It's not like people won't notice the same bright red mid length dress. It's quite a showstopper.

His eyes turn serious, earnest. 'I mean it, you know. I'm happy for you to crash here.'

I need to regain some control here; stop looking into those deep brown eyes and concentrate. Lay some ground rules.

'Okay, but I won't be sharing your bed like last night. We need to keep some emotional distance.'

He leans on the breakfast bar, his strong arms tensing to show off his biceps. I can't stop thinking about that night when he took me over this very breakfast bar.

'You scared you'll catch feelings for me?' He grins.

It's at moments like this it's all too easy to forget he's the serious Cabinet Secretary and believe he's just a gorgeous guy with a flirty streak.

Too late. Feelings have already started brewing. Long ago if I'm honest with myself. I've just never met anyone else like him.

'Nope. Just don't want *you* falling in love with *me*,' I joke back, pretending to be the strong, independent woman I like to think I am. 'I'm a very busy woman.'

He throws his head back and laughs. 'Don't worry. I don't fall in love. I don't have the time.'

That's what I'm worried about.

I GOT out of there as quickly as possible. I shouldn't have done it. Yes, I got the best night's sleep I've had in what feels like forever, but I'm just tangling up my feelings for him. He is the father of my child, and that's all. I can't start dreaming of a happily ever after. The guy said himself he doesn't even want kids. He's going to think I've trapped him. Be pissed off I didn't get an abortion.

Every time I catch sight of him in the office I have fantasies of having sex with him again. Just once. Before I become a big fat whale. Before I kiss goodbye to my single and fancy-free life for good. It's true what they say, you never know what you've got until its gone.

God, the idea of being tied to this urchin growing inside me for the next eighteen years has me feeling nauseous.

'I mean, would it really be the worst idea?' I ask Eloise in the toilets as I change into the fresh outfit she's brought in for me. She's wisely chosen her green leopard print shirt dress. It's the only thing that would have a chance of fitting me.

She snorts a laugh. 'Having sex with your baby daddy? Well, at least you know you can't get pregnant. Again.'

I chuckle a laugh. 'Very true. I am ridiculously horny though.'

Just the thought of being able to trail my fingertips down his muscled chest again has me verging on dribbling.

'But...' she warns with a wag of her finger, 'he could always actually look at your stomach and realise it's gotten bigger.'

'Why, can you tell?' I ask, exiting the cubicle and staring at my reflection in the mirror in a moment of panic.

I suck in my stomach. I must get a hold of myself before I'm having to be crane lifted from the building.

'No, but you will soon.'

It's like I have a loud ticking clock reminding me that time is running out. My life will be over soon.

'All the more reason to do it now. Get it out of my system.' I'm justifying it to myself more than to her.

'I mean, it's up to you.' She goes behind me and zips me up. 'But don't say I didn't warn you when it gets complicated.'

'It's already complicated,' I counter. 'This part isn't. He will have no problem separating sex from emotions. The man has no heart.'

'What about you? Are you going to be able to separate sex from feelings?'

I sigh. Too late for all that. I'm blaming it on the hormones though. As soon as I deliver this child I'll be back to thinking rationally.

'I already fancy the fuck out of him and I'm having his baby. So what's the harm?'

Arthur

I've found myself walking past her desk far more than I should. I know it's stupid, but there's just something about her that seems to attract me towards her like a magnet. Not that she wants to explore it. She made that pretty clear this morning when she told me to keep my hands off her. Probably for the best, I don't have time for those sorts of complications anyway.

I let myself in at home, throwing my satchel to the floor. I sigh, kick off my shoes and then spot her on the sofa. Charlotte. She came again.

Talk about mixed messages.

She stands up and walks over to me, not saying a word, her expression unreadable.

I remain standing, not sure where she's going with this. She smiles, opening up my suit jacket, slipping her warm delicate hands in and around my waist.

Woah.

I look down into her hazel eyes, which still seem unsure. What is with this woman? I thought she wasn't interested.

She presses her face into my shirt. 'You look like you've had a tough day,' she says, her words vibrating against my chest.

I close my eyes for a second, savouring her being so close. Letting myself relax into her warmth. She might change her mind in a second.

'You could say that.'

She leans back to look up at me. Her eyes draw me in, something in them is raw and vulnerable. I know I shouldn't, but I stare at her lips, desperate to feel them on mine again. God, what I'd do for one more taste.

She lifts onto her tip toes, her lips almost on mine. Her gaze lifts, seeking for permission. I close the short distance, my arms crushing her to me. I kiss the fucking life out of her, scared she'll change her mind any moment.

She pulls back and I feel a sharp pain in my chest at the distance. Please don't say she's changing her mind.

'Just sex,' she whispers, eyes darker than a second ago. 'No feelings.'

She's finally speaking my language.

She pushes my suit jacket off my shoulders, dropping it to the floor. Then she's at my shirt buttons, her frantic hands desperate to feel my skin. I reach round to find the zip of her dress, yanking it down, as my mouth drops onto her shoulder. I lick and suck her skin like nectar to a starving man. I pull the dress down to her waist, my hands tucking into her stomach to press it down. She freezes.

'Are you okay?' I ask.

'Yeah fine.' She grabs my hand and puts it over her breast. 'Just feeling a bit bloated.'

I grin back at her. She's so unbelievably cute.

8

Monday 21st September

Charlotte – 23 Weeks Pregnant

*W*ell damn. This was a good idea. Two weeks of non-stop sex. We've done it all around the apartment, even on the balcony overlooking the Thames. I feel like I can't get enough of him. Which is a problem. I was sure by now I'd be sated and have enough in my spank bank to last a lifetime. But it's like every time we do it it's bittersweet, another reminder that this baby is going to ruin everything. Once we stop I'll probably never have sex again.

I feel bad blaming the baby for all of this, but it's my reality. There goes my life in London. Back home I'll be the disgraced single mother I promised myself I'd never be. God, what if the baby is a big bastard like him and I'm left with a gaping big hole of a baggy vagina? I shudder at the thought of it.

The hardest thing of all is that he's made sure the fridge is stocked with plenty of Maltesers and other carby snacks that I know he doesn't eat himself. A big beautiful specimen of a man like that doesn't get built by that kind of food.

Him being sweet is having my hormones confuse everything. God, if he could just fall in love with me. It would be so much easier.

But I already know a man like that is only in love with his job. He told me himself.

Tonight is the last time. I know I've said that the last few times, but it *has to stop*. I'm getting addicted. That and I can't suck my tummy in any longer. Damn those delicious snacks.

I'm on top with his sheets wrapped around my stomach, his hands on my waist as I ride him. I savour the feeling of fullness, so *so* close to orgasm I can feel the tingles beginning to crawl up my spine. That's when... I feel it. A weird dropping sensation in my stomach. As if I've just gone down a dip on a rollercoaster. What the hell? I look down to see if he's noticed anything, his eyes are wide open. Shit.

'What the hell was that?' he asks, his eyes practically bulging out of their sockets.

'Err...'. I quickly hop off him and wrap the blanket closer around myself. Was that the baby kicking for the first time? ... while I'm having sex with its father? Far too gross to contemplate. 'I don't know.'

I look away from him, my mind racing. I need to think of something and quickly. But I was so close to an orgasm, my brain is scrambled.

He touches my chin, turning me to look at him. Concern is etched all over his face. It makes my heart hurt. Once he finds out he'll never look at me like that again.

'What is it? Are you feeling unwell?' He slips his other hand under the cover onto my stomach.

That's when it happens again. Definitely more like a kick this time. His eyes go, as if by slow motion, from my stomach up to my face. Sweat prickles on my neck. This isn't good, any dignity I had left from telling him is gone.

He roughly yanks away the blanket exposing my swollen belly. It's still far more *I've eaten two Christmas dinners* than pregnant, but it's big for me. He grips at it with both hands, staring, mouth agape. There's no escaping this.

'Are you...? Could you be...?' He swallows, his eyebrows bunched. 'Charlotte, what is happening right now?'

'I...' I push his hands away and stand up, grabbing at my dress on the floor. 'I have to go.'

I need to get out of here. Have a chance to think clearly.

'Charlotte.' He sits up properly, the muscles in his stomach tightening deliciously. 'What the hell is going on?'

'I have to go,' I repeat again, tying my navy ruffle waist wrap dress around myself hastily.

He jumps out of bed just as I'm putting my black patent stilettos on.

'Not until you explain what just happened.' He looks more furious now, a vein on his neck throbbing. It's easier to be angry with him when he's like this.

'I'll explain another time.' I turn, attempting to flee again.

Turns out when it comes down to it its more humiliating than anything to admit I'm pregnant. It weirdly feels all of my fault.

He grabs my arm, yanking me back. 'You'll explain right fucking now!' he shouts, his cheeks red.

My chin wobbles, tears springing to life behind my lids.

'I'm sorry,' I say on a sob.

He softens slightly. 'Sorry for what?'

I sit down on the edge of the bed. I have to say it sometime. The game is up. 'I'm pregnant.'

He pales, staring at me with wide eyes for countless silent minutes. Unbearable minutes. Minutes I wish I were dead.

'Wow, I'm so sorry.' He shakes his head in disbelief. 'I didn't realise you were involved with anyone else.'

Oh my god. This is awkward.

I look up at him, torn between the waves of shame washing over me and knowing I shouldn't feel them at all.

'I'm not. It's yours.'

I brace myself for him to start shouting, but what I really don't expect is for him to start laughing. I stare incredulously back at him.

'Very funny. We've only been fucking for two weeks.'

My heart shrivels in my chest. Shit, he thinks this happened within the last two weeks. Has he completely forgotten the first time?

'You don't believe me?' I can't hide the hurt from my voice. I never *ever* wanted to be in a position where the father of my child didn't believe the baby was his. I'm such a cliche.

'I just think you must be wrong.' He nods, blinking rapidly, as if adamant about his decision.

My pulse fastens, rage flooding my system. Fuck him. I'm not being made out to be some slag.

'You know what?' I stand up, grabbing my bag. 'Maybe I am mistaken. Because I thought you had to be a fucking man in order to put a baby in someone's stomach and last time I checked you were just a selfish excuse of a human being!'

I run from the apartment, tears streaming down my face.

I don't stop until I'm near the tube. Well, that went... terribly.

Tuesday 22nd September

Arthur

I didn't sleep at all last night. Pregnant. Fucking pregnant. I've been shagging a pregnant woman? I suppose now that I've sat down and thought about it her tits have got bigger and she did seem slightly larger around the waist and hips, but not enough for me to expect she's pregnant. That's the last thing I would have guessed. The way she eats it was no surprise she was getting bigger. I just figured she'd fallen off the diet wagon.

She says its mine. Could it really be from that one night all those months ago? I googled it and you only start to feel the baby move past sixteen weeks. Is that why she got the job at Whitehall? To be close with me? Has the whole thing been a set up from the very beginning? Trap a rich successful man like me with a baby. Get set up for life.

But even as I think it, I know that's not Charlotte. She's just not like that. She's pure. Almost verging on naive. That's one of the things I like about her most. Fuck, do I like her? Or do I just enjoy fucking her? Having company? Someone to sleep next to me.

So I'm waiting at her desk the next morning with a decaf coffee and a croissant. I've already been waiting a while. Maybe she's called in sick. Couldn't bear to face me.

She finally rounds the corner, looking terrible. Her eyes are tired, red rimmed from what I imagine is a night full of crying; someone accusing you of being a loose woman will do that to you. Her skin is grey from what looks like exhaustion.

'Arthur,' she says when she spots me. She gulps and makes her way over, almost falling over. I catch her just in time. She feels weak and fragile in my arms.

'Have you eaten this morning?' I ask. It comes out more of an accusation.

She snatches the croissant from my hands and takes a bite.

'Now I have,' she snaps.

'Aren't your house mates looking after you?' I lower my voice and move closer to her. So close that her flowery perfume creeps up my nose. 'Do they know?'

She shrugs. 'They know. They just don't really care. They're more worried about finding a new roommate.'

I narrow my eyes at her. 'Why would they be finding a new roommate? Where are you going?'

She sits down, sipping her coffee. She recoils, twisting her lips. 'Ugh, is this decaf?'

'Yes,' I say through gritted teeth. As if I'm going to give a pregnant woman caffeine. 'Where are you going, Charlotte?' I'm losing my temper with her. It's taking all of my restraint not to strangle her.

'I'm allowed one nice coffee a day.'

'Where, Charlotte?' I practically growl. 'Stop avoiding the question.'

The woman is infuriating.

She looks around quickly to check no one is listening. 'I plan to move home to either my mum or dads when the baby is born.'

I suppose that's a rational decision. Get all the support she can. I hear babies are hard work.

'Are they local?'

She scoffs. 'Depends if you think Devon is local.'

'Devon? Fucking Devon?' I've raised my voice so high people are stopping to stare. I take her arm and guide her into Roger's empty office.

'This baby is mine, right?' I say as soon as the door is shut.

She folds her arms across her chest and rolls her eyes. 'Oh, so now you've started to believe me, have you?'

'Hey, don't pretend for one second that you've been honest with me from the beginning,' I snarl. 'We've been sleeping together for two weeks and you've never once found a time to tell me.'

Her face falls, her eyes vulnerable again. Shit, I hate making her look like that. It makes my chest tight.

'I meant to. I just...'

'You just what?' I snap, unable to hide my irritation. This woman has just walked in and fucked my life over.

She sighs fiddling with her necklace. 'I wanted to enjoy myself before having to come crashing down into reality.'

I suppose I can understand that. Last night I was busy enjoying myself. This morning I'm discussing my child with the woman carrying it. Could it be that this was as much a surprise to her as me? It seems to be the case.

'How far gone are you?'

'Twenty-three weeks. Too late for an abortion,' she adds, as if I was going to ask her to consider it.

'Jesus, you're over halfway through.' I grip my hair in my hands, just to have something to hold onto. My life is spinning out of control.

'I'm sorry, but I just couldn't consider an abortion. But you don't have to be involved if you don't want to be. It's totally fine.'

I stare back at her in disbelief. 'Are you fucking joking?

Of course I'm going to be involved. Which is why you're not moving to fucking Devon.'

I need to calm down and stop swearing, but damn if the caveman in me isn't coming out. She's not taking my baby away from me. Sure I might not even want it, but it's here now and I'm not letting her get away.

'Really?' she snorts, 'It's my only option.'

'No, it's not. You'll move in with me.'

'Sorry, what?' She stares back at me, shaking her head.

I'm shocked myself. I hadn't considered it five minutes ago. Now I'm sure with every fibre of my being it's the right thing to do.

'We get on well enough and you know how much I work. If I'm to see this baby at all you'll have to live with me. That and at least I can look after you, make sure you're eating and not commuting every day on an empty stomach.'

'Be careful,' she warns. 'You're starting to sound like you care.'

I grab her chin and force her to look up at me. Scared, vulnerable hazel eyes meet mine.

'I care. I'm not a heartless bastard.' Even as I say it I'm not sure that I'm not.

'I'll have to think about it,' she says, chewing on her lip.

I let my hand fall. Yeah, like she has loads of options.

'Fine, you think about it. But when you realise it's the best plan, I'll be waiting on the second floor.'

9

Charlotte

'He's such an arrogant arsehole,' I tell Eloise over the phone at work. If Roger catches me he'll no doubt go ballistic. He's a real task master. It doesn't help that baby brain has kicked in and I keep forgetting stuff.

'I mean, he is right though,' she tries to reason. 'You get that don't you?'

I sigh. 'Yes and the practical person in me says it makes sense. He's down the road from work, I like his apartment, I love his penis.'

She snorts a laugh.

'But the irrational baby hormone part of me wants to punch him in the face. He basically inadvertently accused me of lying when I said the baby was his last night.'

'You do have to remember that the first night was months ago now.'

'Regardless. It just shows how we still don't know each other. If he knew me at all he'd know I'm not like that.'

'Well then that's the perfect reason to move in with him. Get to know him. Let him get to know you.'

I know she's right. I just don't know if I'm ready to uproot my life even further. My back has really started to ache though. A shorter trip home each night does sound nice.

'Plus, this way I don't lose you to Devon, so you know; win, win.'

Arthur

I still haven't heard from her after lunch when I get an internal post envelope labelled *strictly private and confidential*. That's strange. I normally get hand delivered documents of this security level. I pop open the envelope and reach in.

I pull out a baby scan. Shit. Attached to it is a post it.

'We accept.'

I can't hide the grin from exploding on my face. I remove the post it and look at the scan picture. That's my baby. Shit, that's crazy. You can see its little legs and what looks like a giant head. Must have a huge brain like its daddy. Shit, I'm going to be a daddy. That's insane.

I look at the date. 1st September. I count back the three months. That does seem to be around the first time. Not that I could be certain. But... well, I do trust her. I don't think she's a liar.

This is my baby and I intend to step up to the plate.

Charlotte

That's how I find myself walking into his flat later that evening. I nearly pass out in shock when I find him already sat on the sofa. He smiles, as if waiting for me. My stomach flips inside out. We're going to have an awkward chat. I can feel it.

'What are you doing here at this time?'

He smiles. 'I thought we needed to sit down and have a chat.'

I knew it.

The most we've talked about these past few weeks is how he got the bump on his nose; fell of a horse as a child—a posh boy injury.

'Right.' I sigh, dumping my bag and kicking off my heels. Everything aches. I sit down, stretch out my back and wait for him to talk.

He takes a deep breath, a grave expression on his face. 'I think we should get married.'

I cough, caught completely off guard. 'Sorry, what? You think what?'

He's lost his fucking mind.

'I think it's the most logical step.'

'Why?' I yawn in his face, unable to suppress the fatigue. I am *not* rested enough for this conversation.

'Because we're having a baby. I'm a well-known man in politics. It could be a scandal if I have a baby out of wedlock with a woman I barely know, not least one that is also employed as a PA in my office. But if we announce that we married a while ago in secret the press won't have much to run with.'

I stare back at him, open mouthed. Is he fucking serious right now? He's just worried about his bloody political image.

'Sorry, but less than twenty-four hours ago you didn't even believe you're the father. And now you want to *marry me?*'

He nods. 'I just think it's logical.'

Just how every girl imagines her marriage proposal; unromantic and *logical.*

I shake my head. 'But I don't want to get married. I only want to get married if I'm in love.'

He smiles, as if he finds me adorable. Probably because he doesn't believe in love. God, we're so different. Yes I might have divorced parents, but I still believe every person has a soul mate out there. Clearly he's not mine.

'Think of it as a marriage of convenience then.'

God, he's so old fashioned. I'm in a Jane Austen novel.

I bark a laugh. 'Err, no. I'm not going to marry you. Especially not if it's just so you can save face. I've told you I can disappear to Devon. There's no need for me and this baby to be an embarrassment for you.'

That's the last thing I want to be. And press? I've never bloody heard of the man. I think he's giving himself too much credit. The press would likely yawn and write something about a Love Island contestant.

He takes my hand. 'You're not. I'm just trying to do the right thing.'

'According to who?' Damn, I sound mad. 'Your boss? Society? Because you're sure as hell not trying to do right by me and the baby. That's not what I want.'

'Okay, I'm sorry.' He sighs, running his hand through his hair.

It's so curly by the end of the day. I've loved running my hands through it, but now I don't think it would be appropriate.

'I didn't mean to offend or upset you,' he continues. 'God, that's the last thing I want to do.'

He's made everything awkward now. Or I have... one of us definitely has.

'But I will move in. If that's still okay.'

He beams back at me, his mood changing like a swift wind. 'Good. Actually, I want to show you something.'

He takes my hand and leads me down the corridor, past his bedroom until we're at another door I've never noticed before. He opens it to a small office.

'This can be the baby's bedroom.'

I turn to him confused. 'You mean *my* bedroom.' He doesn't seriously think I'm going to continue to shag him, does he?

He frowns. 'No, you'll be in my room. With me.'

I narrow my eyes back at him. 'I'm sorry, but I think you've got things confused. Yes, I'll be moving in. But no, we won't be shagging anymore.'

He raises one eyebrow. 'Charlotte, we've been screwing the last few weeks. We're having a baby together. You're moving in. Tell me why you'd be suddenly shy about sleeping in my bed?'

Well, when he puts it that way I suppose it does make sense. It's just unclear whether he wants to continue our weird *no strings* relationship. There are clearly strings now. It could get very messy with our strings tangled beyond repair.

'I just... maybe we're better off as friends. I don't want it to get overly complicated.'

He tucks some hair behind my ear. 'We got overly complicated a long time ago.'

Saturday 26th September

Charlotte

It's going to get complicated. Sleeping beside him is only going to let me gaze at his perfect face and feel his body warmth, but not reach out and snuggle into it. We went to bed with no kisses or naughty business so I'm assuming now I'm pregnant he doesn't want me anymore.

Today Arthur is introducing me to his parents. And telling them I'm pregnant. He tells me not to worry but I can tell that he's concerned by the way he's scratching his neck and tensing his shoulders. If he's troubled than I definitely should be.

I find him staring at me as I put my navy coat with flower embroidered arms on. Does he think it's too much?

'What?' I can't help but grin, feeling self-conscious from his gaze.

'I just can't believe I didn't notice before.' He smiles in wonder, comes over and strokes my stomach with his enormous hands. It feels strange to be so intimate. I know we've slept together, but this feels different. It's sweet, not sexy.

'You're a busy man.'

He nods. 'I am indeed. Which is why we need to get this over and done with.'

WE PULL up at a London townhouse in Chelsea, far from the suburban semi-detached I grew up in.

'You're like really rich, then?' I ask with a gulp, looking up at the impressive four stories. It's literally like I've been dropped into *Made in Chelsea*.

He rolls his eyes and performs a perfect parallel park. It's weird how sexy I find that.

'Come on.'

He jumps out of the car, runs round to my side to open the door and takes my hand, leading me to the door.

I get such a rush every time he takes my hand. It feels like I'm his. I wish mine weren't so sweaty, but I'm dreading this.

It strikes me that we haven't discussed our relationship status. They're bound to ask. I'll have to just let him take the lead. I gulp, the panic making my mouth dry.

A man in his early seventies opens the door. Judging from the similar angular jaw it's his dad, the only major difference his salt and pepper hair. He's good looking for an older man.

'Hi!' he says with a warm smile. 'You must be Charlotte.'

'I am.' I nod as he shakes my hand and kisses me on the cheek. A charmer just like his son.

'Pleasure to meet you.'

We bustle into the warmth inside. I follow him down a corridor and then down a set of steps into a huge open plan basement kitchen and lounge. On the sofa is a woman, probably in her sixties. She's thin and the way she sits ramrod straight makes her look regal. She has a Chanel jacket on from their latest show. Fashionable too.

'Hi,' I awkwardly wave.

Arthur smiles. 'Mum, this is Charlotte.'

She raises her hand for me to shake in such a way I wonder if she wants me to kiss the back of her hand. Okay, so she's not as friendly as her husband. That's fine. I lean forward and shake it. Oooh, strong grip too. Nearly crushed my knuckles.

We sit down on the sectional sofa. It's nowhere near as comfy as Arthurs.

'So,' she says clapping her hands together, as if conducting a board meeting. 'You wanted us to meet Charlotte. Am I to assume there's been a proposal?'

Oh god, how embarrassing. She's expecting a ring, not a baby.

He smiles at me, humour in his eyes. 'I did propose, but she turned me down.'

His mother's eyes nearly bulge out of their sockets. 'Why on *earth* would you refuse my son?'

'I—' I start, looking to him for help, forehead sweating. Way to throw me to the sharks.

'That's not important,' he says quickly. 'The reason we're here is that we're... expecting a baby.'

His dad pales, all colour rinsing from his face so quick I fear he'll faint. His mum just remains very still, while what looks like a million clogs turn behind the scenes.

'A baby? How long have you been together?' Her eyes narrow in suspicion. It's clear she's trying to tamper down her rising temper. Her face is growing red, even though she still remains stoic, her hands clenched together so tightly they're turning white.

'Not long,' he answers vaguely, avoiding her direct eye line. 'That's why she said no. She doesn't want us to get married just because of the baby.'

She starts breathing heavily. A rash blooms across her neck. Shit, I hope she's not having some kind of allergic reaction.

'I'm sorry, darling, I'm just having trouble processing this.' She clutches at her temples like a migraine is forming. 'I assume it wasn't planned?'

We both shake our heads. It's pretty obvious it wasn't. I feel like a sixteen-year-old child being chastised, not a thirty-one-year-old.

'How far along are you?' His dad asks, looking towards my stomach.

Is he asking because he wants me to get rid of it?

I swallow, my tongue quivering. 'I'm twenty-three weeks.'

'Jesus,' his mum exclaims, losing her cool. 'And this is the first we learn about it?'

Arthur rolls his eyes. 'Yes, Mother. It's still pretty new. We're just getting used to it ourselves.' Thank god he didn't tell her he only just found out himself. Then she'd really despise me.

'And this is what you want?' she asks him, her face crinkled up in revulsion.

'Yes, Mother,' he says through gritted teeth. 'Obviously it's not ideal, but we're making the best of the situation.'

That is what he's doing isn't it? Just making the best of a bad situation. I clutch my bump protectively. We don't want to be referred to as a situation. This is my worst nightmare.

'I did tell Arthur that he didn't have to be involved if he didn't want to be,' I offer, wanting to explain that I gave him a get out.

She rolls her eyes. 'Yes, but *you* are the one who made the decision to keep the pregnancy. He's hardly going to be able to turn you away now, is he? Not much of a choice.'

'Mother,' he warns, narrowing his eyes at her. 'Be nice.'

'I'm sorry,' she says, sounding anything but. Her rash is climbing to her jaw line now. She stands up and begins to pace. 'I'm just finding it hard to adapt to you being trapped by a *random* woman we know nothing about.'

'She's not a random woman,' he snaps jumping up to stand. 'And if you're not happy for us, that's fine. I suggest you either get on board or lose us all together.'

He takes my hand. 'Come on.'

I look back apologetically as he pulls me out. I don't want to come between him and his parents. Even if his mother is the devil incarnate.

When we get in the car I burst into tears, no longer able

to contain the damn of emotion brewing in my chest. These hormones are making me unhinged. I never normally cry. Well, I mean obviously during sad films... and some commercials, but never in front of people. Not even when I was eleven and my parents were getting divorced.

'Hey,' he soothes, rubbing my arm. 'Don't worry about them. It's a new situation. People are going to be shocked and have opinions. Just ignore them.'

There he goes calling us a situation again. He doesn't realise he's the one hurting me. Thing is, I don't even blame him.

Monday 28th September

Arthur

Well meeting my parents couldn't have gone worse. She's been so low since. It's only a matter of time before the press get wind of it so I've asked my PI to investigate her. Just purely so I know if she's holding back any skeletons in the closet. Just the usual background checks I'd do on anyone I chose to directly employ.

Reggie, a short thin man in his fifties, walks into my office with a confident handshake.

'Let's get straight to it, shall we?' I say as soon as he's sat down in front of me.

'Right.' He takes out his notebook. 'Her background check came back completely clean. A few funny pictures on her Instagram but apart from that she's very normal.'

I release a breath I didn't realise I was holding. Thank God for that.

'Her last relationship was over a year ago,' he continues.

'A Joshua Moore. Ended amicably.'

That's good news too.

'The only thing I could find...'

Oh shit. Just when I thought it was going well.

'Is that her parents had a pretty volatile relationship.'

I nod. That's not a shock to me.

'She did say they divorced.'

He grimaces. 'Yes, but we're not talking a bog-standard divorce here. I'm talking police being called on several occasions. Finding them intoxicated and screaming at each other.'

Shit. Poor Charlotte. It's hard to imagine that she's gone through that. She seems so well rounded. I think of a little Charlotte being brought up around such vicious rows.

That means they'll be police records. This won't look good if it gets out.

'But,' he continues, 'I have to say that for a woman who grew up in such a hostile environment she's done very well for herself. A degree, a steady job. No debt.'

'Thanks. I appreciate you being so thorough.'

Well, this has left me in a conundrum. I still have time to discuss this with her, the news hasn't leaked to the press, yet. They normally request a comment first. I'm sure they'll have lots of questions the nosy bastards. Like my private life has anything to do with how I do my job. Still, I'm going to have to think about how I can broach this with her. It's bound to come up at some point.

She's already so down after meeting my parents, I can't land this on her too.

No, I'll do something nice instead. I buzz through to my PA Rachel.

'Rachel, can you please find me the interior decorator I used for the flat? I have another job for her.'

10

Thursday 1st October

Charlotte – 24 Weeks Pregnant

*A*rthur has been in and out of my office all day and I don't know what's happened to me, but I have the major horn. His broad shoulders, strong jaw, the luscious hair with the curl to it. That man is sex on legs. I know I've been trying to uncomplicate things by not having sex with him, but damn, why does he have to be such a big piece of man candy?

And he's so powerful. It just oozes out of every pore. So serious, with that frown that brings his eyebrows together and wrinkles his forehead. He's going to have a huge Botox bill in a few years. He takes his work so seriously. Even that turns me on.

Every time he looks my way and smiles, it's as if we share a secret. I mean, I know we share a baby, but this is something more. Something that makes me feel connected to him and makes me want to purr deep down in my belly like a pussy cat.

I've found myself squeezing my thighs together to try and get some sort of small release. At one point I even considered going into the bathroom just so I could touch myself. Can you even imagine?! In a government building! I'm on the crazy train. Toot toot!

When I get home I can't help but punish myself further by watching Fifty Shades of Grey. Damn that Jamie Dornan is hot. The things I'd do to him. Not that he has a patch on Arthur.

He arrives home just as the film is finishing. He gives me that secret smile again and I swear, my knickers set fire. Before I know what I'm doing I stand up, walk over to him, and use his belt to pull him towards me.

His eyes widen in shock. I revel in having the upper hand in the situation for once. Everything else in my life feels so out of control. This is the one thing I know. Him and me equals hot sex.

I keep eye contact as I undo his belt, then his top button and zipper. I slide my hand in to find him already hard as rock. There he is. The penis with the killer sperm.

His eyes are so unsure, flitting from one side to the other. I feel strong and powerful, so I drop to my knees and drag his trousers and boxer shorts down to his ankles. I take him in my mouth, too eager to go slow.

'Jesus, Charlotte,' he hisses, his thighs tensing under my hands.

Feeling encouraged I suck harder, allowing him further down my throat. Sure, it's hard to breathe through my nose and my knees are already aching like hell but I persist. Ultimately I want to make him happy. That and I'm getting as much from this as he is. I don't know what's come over me, but I need this. Need to forget I'm pregnant and enjoy myself. Feel desired.

After several minutes I've started to lose momentum. I'm desperate for him to finish. All enthusiasm has long fallen behind the crushing fatigue and jaw ache. I'm just about to stop when he speaks.

'Yes, Charlotte. I'm so close. *So* close.'

Well okay. If he's that close I can't stop now; I don't want to be cruel. I persevere like the total champ that I am. That is until I start to feel lightheaded, a bit dizzy.

The next thing I know I'm on the floor. I look around. What the hell happened? I look up to see Arthur running around with his limp cock flapping about.

'Oh my god, you're awake,' he says when he spots me. 'Where's the book?'

'The book?' I repeat, still feeling dazed.

'The book! The *BOOK!* Your pregnancy book thing! With the numbers to call!'

I try to sit up, but I still feel wobbly. 'Oh. Um... in my bag?'

He runs to get it, then he's back with me, helping me to sit up. I feel so weak and wiped out.

'How are you feeling?' He checks over my face, cupping my cheeks in his giant hands.

'A bit dizzy, but okay.' *More embarrassed than anything.*

He punches in the number on his phone, hands it over to me and then goes to get a glass of water.

'Hello, maternity ward,' a cheery female voice answers.

'Um, hi. I think I just passed out?' I mean, I still don't know for sure what happened. My head is all over the place.

'Okay and how many weeks pregnant are you?' she enquires.

'I'm twenty-four weeks.'

God, I'm still so far away from delivery. What if I've done something to hurt the baby? I'll never forgive myself. All because I was bloody horny.

'Okay and what were you doing right before you fainted?'

Arthur hands me a glass of water.

'Umm...' I look to Arthur in wide eyed panic. I have to lie. There's no way I'm telling her the truth. 'I was just... getting up from the sofa.'

'Really?'

Damn, she doesn't sound convinced.

'Because fainting just from standing is very rare. Especially this early on in the pregnancy.'

She's got me there.

'Tell her the truth,' Arthur whispers with an encouraging nod. 'It might be important.'

How the hell would it be relevant?

I sigh, already feeling my cheeks heat. 'Okay, I was actually on my knees at the time.'

'Okay and what were you doing on your knees?'

What do you bloody think I was doing? Nosy bitch.

'Um... I was...'

'Yes?' She encourages. 'Please rest assured that anything you tell me is to be kept strictly confidential. I'm not here to judge.'

'Okay.' I take a deep breath. 'I was giving my...' God, how do I describe Arthur? He's not my boyfriend. 'The father of my child a... a blow job.'

Arthur covers his face with his hands. Only I could get myself into this mess.

Silence greets me on the other end of the phone. Is she still there? Maybe she's passed out from shock.

'Hello?'

'Yes.' She clears her throat. 'Sorry, I'm here.' It's clear in her voice she's trying not to let a giggle escape. Judgy bitch lied. 'Have you felt the baby move since?'

I nod even though she can't see me. 'It's moving right now.'

Arthur puts his hands on my stomach and smiles back in surprised wonder when he feels it.

'Okay that's good. Keep on counting your kicks and if you could please drop in a urine sample to your GP tomorrow morning. We'll also send you for blood tests and an ECG, just to be safe. But between me and you I think it's just a case of poor circulation mixed with not enough oxygen.' Her tone is amused.

I'm sure all the nurses will have a good laugh tonight. Glad to be of service to the NHS.

I thank her even though that was totally humiliating and hang up.

'Jesus, Charlotte. You nearly gave me a heart attack.' His eyes are wild and jittery. He was genuinely scared. He really does care for this baby. That's good to know.

'I'm the one that passed out. Don't make it out like I did it deliberately.' I don't know why I'm sounding so bitchy.

He frowns. 'I'm not. I just...'

'You just what?' I ask, already dreading the answer.

He takes my hand, a sad smile on his lips. 'I think this is a sign that we should stop all sexual involvement.'

'Involvement?' God, this man is cold. Just when I think he's starting to show some emotion he goes and says that. I had the man's dick in my mouth less than ten minutes ago.

He nods, all matter of fact.

'It's safer all round. Plus you were right before. We shouldn't make things more complicated than they need to be. This baby is going to be hard enough. We don't want to add any complications to that.'

'Oh. Yeah. Of course.'

And just like that my heart which had soared so high, plummets back down to earth.

Friday 2nd October

Arthur

Well last night was a weird one. I have no idea what came over her to suddenly be so randy, but I can't say I wasn't having the time of my life. Until she passed out of course.

The thoughts that were racing through my head had me feeling sick to the stomach. *Would she be okay? Was the baby alright? What if she miscarried?*

It made me realise how invested in this baby I really am. A short while ago I couldn't imagine myself with kids and now the thought of losing one has me gasping for breath, my chest tightening.

It scares me that it's left me so vulnerable. Her pregnancy is completely out of my control and that makes me feel uneasy. It's not that I don't trust her. I know she'd never do something to intentionally harm her or the baby, but something could happen, no fault of her own.

Babies are so small and helpless. Then the thought that I might be worrying about this kid for the rest of my life jumps into my brain. Dammit. I'm not sure I can cope with that level of anxiety.

'There's really no need for me to have the day off,' Charlotte whines the next morning as she eats her croissant with fruit that I insisted upon.

'I don't care. It's happening. You're to lay on that sofa and relax. Understood?'

She rolls her eyes but I can see the slightest hint of a smile.

'I still need to drop in my urine sample.' She's so cute how she goes red at just the word urine. How she's going to feel giving birth in front of me I don't know.

'I'll drop it in for you,' I offer. Any excuse for her to try and leave the flat.

'Are you sure?' She squirms uncomfortably. When is she going to realise she's not a burden to me?

I roll my own eyes. 'Charlotte, would you stop being so immature and give me your urine.' A sentence I never thought I'd say.

She snorts a laugh. 'Okay.'

She sighs but goes to the bathroom and emerges a few minutes later with a tiny plastic container of urine.

'Have fun,' she says as she hands it over.

I put it into my trouser pocket, wait with raised eyebrows until she settles back down onto the sofa and then leave for the clinic. I'm almost there when I feel a sort of wetness. I look down and follow it to my pocket. Shit.

I take out the pee bottle and peer at the lid. The stupid woman hasn't done up the bottle properly. Her pee has leaked all over me! Dammit. I don't have time to walk home before my next meeting. I toss the sample into a nearby bin and power walk the rest of the way.

Damn that Charlotte. I swear she'll be the death of me.

I've barely walked in when Roger approaches me, face like thunder.

'That PA you recommended to me has called in sick. So thanks for that.'

I grit my teeth. The idiot has no idea that she's pregnant with my baby and I'm the one that forced her to stay home.

'I don't have time for this Roger.' I turn and walk away before I pummel him in the face.

'Can anyone smell wee?' I hear him ask in the distance.

Yep. The absolute death of me.

Monday 5th October

Charlotte – 25 Weeks Pregnant

After what I'm referring to as *'pee gate'* happened Arthur hasn't been able to look at me the same again. To say he was mad would be the understatement of the year. Oh well, it served him right for being so bossy and demanding I take the day off.

His PA had to run out and buy emergency trousers, so he was late for his meeting and then apparently they kept asking if anyone could smell pee. He was mortified but I couldn't stop laughing, even if I never realised my wee smells. I'm not sure he's ever going to forgive me.

Roger's had the arse with me since. He's a bloody psycho. One minute he's saying I haven't given him some documents, only to find them ten minutes later. I'm walking on constant eggshells. It's messing with my head.

When I get home from work the following week there's the unmistakable smell of another woman's perfume. It's pretty pungent, a tangy smell of florals mixed with spice.

My stomach recoils at the idea of someone else being in what's supposed to be my home. Why would a woman be here?

I go into the bedroom to see if anything is out of place.

Nope. All seems fine here. I open the wardrobe and all of my clothes have been organised by colour like in those fancy celeb's wardrobes. He must have paid someone to come and organise me. All my handbags are lined up prettily. With no room to unpack, I've been living from suitcases since I officially moved in. I didn't feel right taking his things out to make space for my own.

Bless him to think to do this. That must be it. He knows being unorganised was driving me mad. I wonder where he's put half his clothes.

I call him and he picks up after three rings.

'Hi.'

'Hi, thanks for getting my stuff put away.'

'One less thing for you to worry about.'

I smile, imagining the cocky smile which I'm sure is on his face right now.

'Did you pay someone specially to do it?' I need to know where this perfume came from. My unsettled stomach and irrational mind is telling me to be worried.

'No. Just our regular cleaner.'

I love how he says *'our'* regular cleaner. Like I really live here. Like I'm really part of his life.

But then... surely I'd have smelt the cleaner before if she wore perfume that strong? Or maybe it's just the pregnancy making my sense of smell more intense? I'm sure I've heard that happens.

Either way I'm sure he's had a woman other than our cleaner here. And that makes me nervous. Far more nervous than I'm comfortable with.

Arthur

'We have a problem,' Sally my PR Officer says, barging into my office.

This must be bad. She'd never normally be so rude.

'What is it?' I snap, turning away from my computer.

She chews on her bottom lip. 'We've just had a national newspaper contact us and ask for a comment.'

I frown. Oh god. Time has run out. It's happening.

'In regard to what story?' I ask, playing for time.

'In regard to you getting one of your employees pregnant.' She raises her eyebrows at me.

'Ah.'

Shit.

Her eyebrows shoot up to her hair line. 'Please tell me this isn't true?' she pleads

'Well... she wasn't my employee when I got her pregnant.'

God, I hate having to discuss my private life with her. This is one reason why I don't date. There's always the risk of someone selling a story on me. The press can always sniff out a scandal and despite how far we've come in this day and age, an unexpected pregnancy for someone in my position is still bad for the government's image. It has people wondering. If I can't organise my personal life, what chance do I have at doing my job right? Even though I am more than bloody capable.

I live and breathe this job and have been a civil servant since university. Not that they'll write any of that of course. They only care about scandalous headlines and selling papers.

'Shit.' She sits down on a chair across from my desk,

pulling her hair away from her face. 'But now she works here?' she asks, desperate for me to elaborate.

I nod. 'She's Roger Fielding's PA. Nothing to do with me at all.'

She sighs. 'We both know that's not how it'll be seen.'

'I know.' I stare out of the window. I knew it was coming, but I still feel sick about it.

'Are you at least engaged to be married?' Her face brightens up at the prospect. 'Or did you marry in secret?'

I shake my head. 'I tried to talk about marriage, but she doesn't want to marry just for my image.'

She rolls her eyes. 'Ugh, trust you to impregnate a hopeless romantic.'

I bristle at her discussing Charlotte. She's not just some idiot, she has her own brain and passionate ideas.

'Well, you'll have to convince her,' she insists, crossing her arms over her chest.

I scoff. She's clearly never met Charlotte. 'I can't just force her.'

'I didn't say *force*, I said convince. This will look a hell of a lot better if we come back tomorrow and say that you're happily engaged.'

I sigh, scrubbing my hands over my face. 'I mean... I can try again.'

'Marvellous.' She stands, making me think the conversation has ended until she adds, 'You know the PM will much prefer it this way. The less scandal we have, the better.'

I nod, even though I'm pissed. How many MP's have been found cheating on their wives and forced to resign? That's a real scandal, not innocently knocking a woman up.

Guess I have some grovelling to do tonight.

11

Charlotte

I might have called Eloise and cried hysterically down the phone about smelling the perfume. I'm sure she was terrified. These damn hormones are seriously changing who I am as a person. That's what scares me most.

I've always looked at highly strung women like my own mother and wondered why they were so crazy. Why they couldn't just walk away from arguments? Now I realise it might be beyond their control. What if I never go back to normal?

She's reassured me that it's probably the cleaner's new perfume and that I should stop worrying. Yeah, like anyone ever stopped worrying just because they were told to.

I'm just wondering if I should order a Chinese when Arthur walks in, carrying what looks and smells like a takeaway.

'Oh my god, you read my mind.' I jump up and grab the bag from him.

I quickly microwave our plates, grab cutlery and then lay it out for us. I open the bag. My heart sinks when I realise it's not your average takeaway. It's grilled chicken, brown rice and asparagus. Ugh, so not what I fancied.

Regardless, I help myself. Okay, so it tastes a lot better than it looks. Still would have preferred a Chinese. He looks on, amused, his lips quirking at the edges.

'So how was your day?' I ask around a mouth of chicken.

He looks down at his plate. 'Interesting.'

My stomach drops. Something happened.

'Oh dear. Why do I get the feeling that's code for shit?'

He puffs a laugh. 'Look, I have to tell you something.'

Oh my god this is it. When he tells me he's had some woman over here, he's running away with her, and that I should move out.

'What is it?' I ask, already feeling so jittery my tongue trembles.

'My PR office had a call from a newspaper. They're printing our story tomorrow.'

Thank god. *Not another woman.*

My mouth gapes open. 'Our story? What do you mean, *our* story?'

He sighs, scratching his neck. 'That you officially work for me and I got you pregnant.'

Well that sounds worse than what actually happened.

'But... but it happened before I worked there.'

He smiles and gives a gentle shake of his head. 'You know as well as I do that it doesn't matter. It'll still be seen as bad for the government. This was what I was scared of.'

'I don't understand. No offence, but you're hardly a celebrity. I'd never seen any article or picture of you before I met you.'

'That's because I keep my head down and get on with my job.'

Realisation settles over me. 'Until I came along and fucked up your life?'

My stomach churns at the thought of it. This good man is going to have his name pulled through the mud because of one night of carelessness. Because we both thought those condoms would work. I've ruined his career. His life probably.

'You haven't fucked up my life,' he says, but I can see behind his eyes that he's so very tired. His soul is tired and I'm the reason for his exhaustion.

'Is there anything I can do to help?'

He smiles and avoids eye contact. 'Actually, there is.' He runs his hands through his hair.

'What is it? Just name it.'

He sighs, sits up straight and then looks me in the eye. 'We could get engaged.'

I frown back at him. Engaged? Not this again.

'Haven't we been through this?'

'Not a proper engagement,' he insists. 'Just an engagement for the public. An engagement of convenience if you will.'

A million thoughts run through my head. *He doesn't love you, he barely likes you. He doesn't want to actually marry you, he just wants to look like less of a douche when that story drops.* But getting engaged, even if fake, is a big deal.

'Will everyone have to think I'm engaged? Eloise? My parents, your parents?'

He nods, chewing his lip. 'I think it's the only way it'll work.'

I mean I suppose I do understand. I would look less of a

slutty single mother in the press. To my old school mates. Everyone I've ever met.

'Okay, I'll do it.'

His eyes light up. 'Seriously?'

'Yeah. Anything to make your life easier.'

'God, you're an amazing woman.' He pulls me closer, enveloping me in a hug.

If only he held real affection for me I wouldn't feel such a burden. Unfortunately I fear the man has no heart to give.

Tuesday 6th October

Arthur

I can't believe she agreed to it so easily. I was sure she'd put up a fight and I wasn't planning on pressurising her into it. I sent Sally a text to let her know that I'd release a statement first thing this morning.

When I wake up I immediately open the front door to my morning delivery of every national newspaper. My face is on most of them. Dammit. There I was hoping for page twelve. Must be a slow news day.

'Cabinet Secretary Knocks Up PA.'

Well fuck, that sounds even worse than it is. I scan over the writing.

'Charlotte Bellswain is expected to be around twenty-five weeks pregnant.'

There's a grainy picture of her walking along the street, the wind blowing her coat away so that her small bump is visible. Dammit. I run my finger over the little bump. How can I feel so much love for a baby I haven't met yet?

I turn the coffee machine on and jump into a hot

shower, letting it soothe my tight muscles. When I get out Charlotte's awake, already reading the papers in just her vest top and pyjama shorts. I can almost see her arse.

'Wowza,' she says, her eyes like a rabbit in headlights.

I still find it adorable how she's so shockable. So un-ruined by the cruel world out there.

'Yep. Don't worry. I'm going to draft a statement this morning.'

She pouts her lips, as if smelling something bad. 'Really? A statement?'

'Yes, why?' Has she changed her mind? Please God no. Not that she doesn't have every right.

'I just think it would look better if we did a picture and a heartfelt post to Instagram.'

'Are you serious?' I snort. Social media? She's crazy.

She glares back at me. 'Remember that I'm the normal general public. I know what we look for. The world wants a love story, not a blanket cold statement. That will just make you look even worse.'

I go into the bedroom and get changed. I suppose she might be right. God knows she's sacrificing enough by agreeing to be fake engaged. She should have some say in how its announced. This will change her life.

I walk back out to find her in a plum wrap dress, her hair still deliciously bed head, not a scrap of make up on. She's still breathtakingly beautiful, all the more for being natural.

'Okay. We'll do your photo thing,' I announce, leaning across the breakfast bar.

Her face lights up. 'Amazing.'

God, I love making her happy. It scares me.

'Come on the sofa.'

I frown but follow, sitting down next to her. She gets her phone out and puts it on selfie mode.

'Don't you want to do your hair and make-up?' I ask. I mean, I thought she wanted to do this so that everyone could coo at her. Not that she doesn't look stunning.

She shrugs. 'The quicker we nip this story in the bud, the better right?'

I nod.

'I mean, unless you think I should?' She scans over herself self-consciously.

I hate that I've made her doubt her beauty. I look at her natural radiance, her skin practically glowing.

'You look perfect.' Never have I spoken a truer sentence.

'Good,' she nods, clearly not believing me by the way she fidgets with her necklace. 'Now shut up.'

She takes my hand with hers but then stops. 'Shit, we don't have a ring.'

My Grandma's voice pops into my head. *Give my ring to the woman you marry. The woman you love like no other.*

'Actually... I kind of have an old one.'

'Sorry?' she asks, narrowing sceptical eyes at me. 'You have an old ring lying around the house?'

I grin. Is she really thinking I'm some Casanova proposing left and right?

'It's not what you think. My grandma gave it to me before she passed, she wanted me to give it to the woman I marry.' I don't include the love bit. Don't want her to get the wrong end of the stick.

She smiles but it's only a small upturn of her mouth. 'Fine, go find it.'

Half an hour later we're sat back down on the sofa, this time with my grandma's solitaire diamond on a gold band fitting perfectly on her finger. She has very delicate hands like my Grandma. I ignore her voice in my head telling me it's a sign.

She takes my hand, intertwining our fingers, and places it on her small bump, Grandma's engagement ring glistening in the light.

'Now act happy,' she instructs. I like it when she's bossy. When she's telling me what she really wants and not what she thinks she should say.

We both beam at the camera while she takes what feels like a hundred pictures from different angles.

She drafts something in her notes and hands it over to me. 'What do you think about this?'

I change it slightly, but overall I'm impressed. She's right. This way seems more personal. I send it via WhatsApp to my phone along with a few pictures to choose from.

I upload two of my favourite pictures. The first is of us both beaming with happiness at the camera, her unique hazel eyes glowing with warmth. The second is my personal favourite. She caught me off guard smiling at her, as if I can't get enough of her. They look so real. The public are going to love her.

We have news! We're over the moon to announce that we're expanding our family early next year. Myself and @charlottefashion couldn't be happier and thank everyone for their well wishes.

I told Charlotte to go through her Instagram as quickly as possible to delete any photos that might be considered risqué. That and any comments about government but luckily she stays away from all of that.

'Okay, I'm going to post it. Are you ready? After this everything changes.'

My stomach jumps around in nervous anticipation.

She smiles and it's so refreshing. She really is a brave woman. Willing to do all this just for me.

'As I'll ever be.'

I press post. It's out there now.

'Now comes the hard part. Telling Eloise and my parents.' She grimaces.

'And mine.' I grin, already considering the fallout from my mum.

Well, she did want us engaged.

Charlotte

I ring Mum straight away.

'Darling,' she answers. 'What's going on? You're on the news.'

'Yeah. Sorry I didn't get a chance to tell you. But we're… getting married.'

'Oh, darling that's fantastic! Phil! Phil!' She shrieks into the background.

My dad is there?

'Charlotte is getting married! Yes of course to the father of the baby!'

I laugh to myself as Arthur himself answers what seem like a hundred calls.

'Why is Dad there?' I ask. Bit suspicious if you ask me. They're supposed to hate each other.

'Oh he just popped round to fit a lightbulb for me.'

That's random. They're normally at each other's throats, not popping around for a cuppa and some home maintenance.

'Oh wait, darling. They've just put a new picture of you both on Good Morning Britain.'

'That quick?' I shriek. Their research department must be amazing. I fumble for the remote control and turn it on. There in HD is our picture and announcement. But they're talking about the second picture. What second picture?

They show the outtake of him smiling down at me. He uploaded that one too, why?

'Listen to them darling.'

Kate Garraway is congratulating us, saying what a lovely couple we make. The other presenters are agreeing, saying he clearly looks smitten. There's some open discussion about how far along I am, when I got pregnant, if it was planned, when we got engaged and how long we've been together. Overall, it's positive.

Arthur hangs up the phone.

'You are a bloody genius,' he says hugging me round the waist. He stoops down to my belly. 'Did you know your mummy is a PR genius?'

I giggle, feeling deliriously happy. I must remember it's not real.

'Oh, I'll let you love birds get back to it,' Mum says, sounding delighted. 'Call me back soon and let me know all the details.'

Now I have to think of a fake engagement story. The good thing about it being fake is I can make it as elaborate as I please.

I hate having to lie to them, but I remind myself that this is for the best long term. Well, that is until he finds someone he actually wants to marry and kicks me and the baby to the kerb. I force the thought to the back of my mind and try to remain positive.

12

Charlotte

I'm barely into work when Eloise accosts me, her gaze accusing, lips pressed flat.

'Char, what the actual fuck?' she demands, far too loudly for an office environment.

'And good morning to you too,' I answer.

'You're engaged now?' she demands, hand on her hip.

'Yes, okay?' I whisper hiss, hating the added extra attention. I've already had everyone staring at me on the way in.

She peeks into Roger's office and when she finds it empty grabs me by both arms and drags me in, slamming the door behind us.

'Okay, cut the bullshit. What's going on?'

I sigh. How is it I can lie to my parents no problem but one look into Eloise's probing gaze and I shrivel like a raisin.

'Okay, it's a publicity thing. It's not real.'

'I knew it!' She does a triumphant fist pump in the air. 'I

knew you weren't going to allow him to pressure you into a real one.'

I hate that she doubted me, and I can't believe she has so little faith in him as a person. That's my baby's father she's talking about. I feel strangely protective of him.

'Whatever. My parents don't even know so you'll have to play along.'

She grimaces, leaning her head to one side. 'How did they react?'

'Well, first off they were in the same house.'

Her eyes widen to twice the size. 'God, why?'

She knows too well how volatile they are together, back when I lived at home I often escaped to her house.

'Apparently he was changing a light bulb.' I roll my eyes.

She shakes her head. 'Okay, let's put a pin in that weird bit of information. What did they say about it all?'

I shrug. 'They sounded pleased. I mean, they think I'm marrying the guy. That I'm living the fairy tale. You promise you won't land us in the shit?'

Eloise is a great friend, but she has been known to spill a secret after a bottle of wine.

She sighs. 'Of course I won't. I just think its shit he's making you do this. All to save face.'

'Well...' I chew on the inside of my cheek, 'to be honest it does kind of look better for me too. Rather than a random unmarried mother.'

She scoffs. 'I didn't realise we were living back in the fifties.'

I raise my eyebrows at her and she sighs. 'Fine, so you're really okay with this?'

'Yes. I just want to get on with my day.'

She smiles, but I know this isn't really over. She's going

to ride me hard about every single decision I make concerning Arthur Ellison.

'Charlotte,' Roger says, walking into the office, his face furious. 'A word please.'

Friday 9th October

Charlotte

Well Roger wasn't impressed with my pregnancy so early on in my employment. Not that I've told Arthur that. I don't want to be the whinny girlfriend, or whatever the hell I am to him. That and he's already so stressed at work, I don't want to add to the pressure.

Besides Roger was being very careful with his words. It was all in the way he said them and how he looked at me with such distaste. I know what he's thinking. That I shouldn't have applied for the job if I knew I was pregnant. I tried to explain I only found out after I'd started work here, but it's pretty obvious from the picture we posted that I'm further along than a few weeks.

I had to tell him my due date and send an email to HR informing them officially of my pregnancy. Then a lady came to see me and make sure that my work desk was comfortable and do a risk assessment. I'm pregnant not disabled.

Anyway, right now I'm in hospital hooked up to an ECG machine, with wires stuck to my chest on the insistence of my midwife.

'And can I ask what you were doing right before you passed out?' The doctor asks, checking his chart.

Oh God, not this again. The nurse on the phone must

not have written it down. I feel bad for thinking so poorly of her.

'I just stood up too quickly.'

He frowns. 'Really? That is concerning. We may have to send you home with a machine. Make sure you're not having any heart arrhythmias.'

Oh God. I don't want to worry Arthur unnecessarily. He's already acting overprotective, making sure I'm eating right. This would send him over the edge.

'No, I really don't think there's any need for that.' I smile, hoping he'll take pity on me.

He shakes his head. 'I'm afraid I have to insist. Unless you were doing something more consistent with a fainting?'

He stares at me expectantly. The nurse is scribbling away on a form.

'Okay, I was on my knees giving my...' I gulp. 'The father of my child a... um, oral sex.'

I couldn't have said that more awkwardly.

His jaw drops open. The nurse stops writing to stare. Both of their mouths quirk up in a smile.

'It's fine.' I shrug on a sigh. 'Go ahead, laugh.'

The nurse starts laughing so hard that she clutches her stomach. The doctor glares at her, but you can tell he wants to laugh too.

He turns to me, trying desperately to be serious. 'I'm afraid we'll have to include this in your official notes.'

I snort. 'Of course you will.'

Thursday 15th October

Charlotte – 26 Weeks Pregnant

Eloise pissed herself laughing and Arthur even found it funny when I told him what happened at the hospital. The nurse proceeded to give me a tour of the maternity wing, giggling non-stop to herself. I really hope I don't get her when I deliver. Fortunately I'm too busy with this damn job and demanding Roger to dwell on it.

Myself and Arthur both get in around the same time every night. The job is bloody killing me. I'm working harder than I ever did at the fashion house and I used to think that was hell. This civil servant shit is brutal. My feet ache, my boobs are heavy and I'm starting to feel a bit sick. Early night for me.

'How was your day?' he asks, scanning over my face and obviously realising it was shit. 'Ah. Cup of decaf coffee?'

I practically growl back at him. Damn decaf. I kick off my shoes and throw myself onto the sofa. I'm already starting to feel like a whale. Today I sneezed and I was so close to wetting myself. I'm sure I shouldn't be at that stage already. Imagine pissing myself at work? It would be mortifying.

'Oh, my friend James is back in town. Wanted to know if we'd go to dinner next Tuesday?'

I perk up at this. Food. I'm already salivating wondering what's on the menu. He keeps forcing all of his healthy food down me.

'Okay. What restaurant?'

'James wants the Italian on Grey's Road. That okay with you?'

'Mmm, Italian. Count me in.' I beam back at him, already googling their menu. What should I have? Pasta or pizza? Whatever I have I want a side of French fries. Followed by a tasty dessert.

I glance up to find him staring at me with a small smile. 'Glad to have made you smile.'

God, when he looks at me like that my heart blossoms. It would be too easy to believe he really cared for me and not just the baby.

'So how do you know James?' I enquire, suddenly nervous at the idea of meeting his friend. Lying to another person.

'We went to uni together. Probably my closest friend. We always catch up when we can.'

This is a big deal. He's introducing me to one of his best friends. God, he'll be introducing me to him as his fiancé. Unless he's told him the truth? No, he swore we wouldn't tell anyone the truth. But then I told Eloise. Not that I've told him that.

'Have you told James our engagement is fake?'

His forehead wrinkles. 'Of course not. We promised not to tell anyone, right?'

'Right,' I nod, my cheeks heating.

He narrows his eyes. 'You haven't told anyone, right?'

'Of course not.' I roll my eyes to look believable. I can't have him find out. He'll think I'm an untrustworthy flaky bitch and I do not want him to lose all faith in me so early in this pregnancy.

13

Saturday 17th October

Charlotte

*A*rthur's always working. Even when he's home he's glued to his phone and laptop. It's really hard to watch on a Saturday, so I've decided to get some fresh air. I'm wandering through a gorgeous boutique baby shop I've stumbled upon, when I see him. I know it's him just from the back of his head, his chocolate brown hair and slim neck. My ex-boyfriend Josh. What the hell is he doing in a baby store?

He turns, heading to the counter with a white baby grow. I try to hide behind a child mannequin but of course he spots me. I'm huge nowadays.

'Charlotte?' He peers behind the mannequin, one eyebrow raised. His face brightens. 'It *is* you.'

I walk around the mannequin. Too late now.

'Hi.' I wave awkwardly.

God, is there ever a good time to run into your ex? When you're pregnant with a man that you barely know it's almost excruciating.

'How are you?' he asks, his green eyes warm. I've missed those eyes. He was such a great guy.

I point down to my stomach. 'Pregnant.'

'So I hear,' he chuckles. 'I couldn't believe it when I saw you on the news.'

How embarrassing. I desperately try to think cooling thoughts and not blush crimson.

'What are you doing here?' I ask him, wishing with everything in me that I looked better today. Didn't have three-day greasy hair scraped back into a severe ponytail and the start of a red spot on my chin. Pregnancy is making me so oily. The only thing I have going for me is my cute outfit of a white band t-shirt tucked into a leopard print mid length pleated skirt and white sneakers.

He must have settled down and got married. That's why we didn't work. He wanted to get married and have kids, but I was too interested in my career. Now look at me. Pregnant with no prospects.

'My sister is expecting,' he answers with a kind smile. 'Thought I'd pick something up for her baby shower.'

He was always the sweetest. He looks damn good too, like he's just been on holiday, his skin tanned and his freckles out on his nose. To think I could have had a baby with this guy, but I was too focused on myself and building my career. Now I'm having one with a guy that's not available emotionally.

'Look, I know you're engaged and everything, but would you like to grab a drink sometime? Catch up?' He looks so hopeful.

'Umm...' Shit, what do I say to that? I doubt Arthur would be impressed, and I wouldn't want to lead Josh on.

'Obviously I mean just a decaf coffee and purely as friends.'

What is it with men wanting me to drink decaf?

God, where's the harm in it really? I feel so lonely living in London. Everyone I know lives in Watford. Before weekends would have been spent surrounded by friends at the local pub gossiping about our week. I could still visit them all, but even the idea of the long train journey has me exhausted. I'd likely just fall asleep on their shoulder when I arrived. It would be nice to know someone else fairly local. And he's always been easy to talk to. We were more friends by the end.

'Yeah, why not.'

Tuesday 20th Oct

Charlotte – 27 Weeks Pregnant

I've felt pretty crap all day. I thought in your second trimester you were supposed to feel amazing? Instead, I had a great first trimester and now I'm feeling shitter by the day. The fatigue is the worst. It's clawed at me all day but I've fought against it. The thought of having to meet Arthur's closest friend tonight has my anxiety through the roof.

He's not back yet so I draw myself a nice relaxing bath and okay... I might nod off for a little while in there. Okay, the truth is I slept way too long and woke up in cold water with only one of my legs shaved. Oh well, I'll just have to wear tights.

I scramble around getting dressed. I really need to invest

in some maternity clothes because nothing bloody fits anymore! Even my wrap dresses are bulging inappropriately. A plain black one will have to do.

I feel like a fat ugly frump as I plaster make up on my oily face to try and look more awake. I layer on lots of jewellery just so I don't look so plain.

I feel like I've aged five years since the start of this pregnancy. It shows too. I swear I've got crow's feet that weren't there before.

God, Arthur is probably repulsed when he looks at me. He'll no doubt be so humiliated introducing dumpy little me to his friend. It's unbelievable to think someone like Arthur would settle for someone like me. I'm so ordinary.

He comes in, late as usual, staring at his watch.

'Shit, sorry I'm so late. I was hoping to jump in the shower, but do you think I'll do like this?'

I look over him. I love his hair by the end of the day. It loses its style and goes to its natural curls. His suit probably cost more than my last month's rent and he fills it so well, all strong defined muscles. I'd climb him like a tree right now if it weren't for the no sex rule.

'You look great. I'm the fat frump everyone's going to stare at.'

I'm not even fishing for compliments. I couldn't feel more low right now. I grab my purse and force a smile.

He frowns down at me. 'You look fabulous.'

I roll my eyes but let him usher me out of the flat, his hand at the base of my back. Whenever he touches me it's like electric currents pulse throughout my body. I don't think he feels it.

When we finally arrive at the dimly lit romantic restaurant I'm twiddling a tissue from my purse. My mum does this when she's nervous. I never wanted to inherit it, but it's funny how calming it feels to fidget out some of my anxiety.

The hostess takes our coats and tells us that our guest is already at the table. I look around for a single guy but can't seem to find one. Instead a woman with long brunette hair starts waving over at us, her gold bracelets jingling with the action. Who the hell is she?

'Ah, there she is,' Arthur says, waving back and pushing me forward by my lower back.

'She?' I ask, already being thrust towards the woman. James is a *woman?* He failed to tell me that.

James stands up and she's as lithe and as long as a supermodel. Damn, maybe she is. She embraces Arthur, squeezing her eyes shut as she crushes her boobs against him. *Alright, that's enough of that.*

'Artie, it's been too long!'

Jealous rage settles in the pit of my stomach. Artie. I hate that. He hasn't told me to call him Artie. I hate her, purely because she's gorgeous, and thin, and I feel like a heifer.

'And Charlotte.' Her ocean blue eyes light up as if I'm the most beautiful woman in the room. Maybe she's an actress. 'It is *such* a pleasure to meet you!'

I smile back but then she's suddenly leaning down and clutching at my bump. Her hands are far too close to my vagina for my liking. *Buy me a drink first.*

'And lovely to meet you too, little one!'

Jesus, we've just met. Don't be talking to my baby. Don't think you have any claim over this baby just because you're besties with its father. It's father that I'm quickly realising I know so little about. How could he have failed to tell me his best friend is a woman?

We get seated as they begin to chatter about old university friends. People called Tabitha, Binky and

Thomas. I know Thomas isn't a posh name, but the way they say it you'd think it was. All *Thooooomaasss.*

I take the time to have a good look over her. She must be Arthur's age, so early forties, but she could easily pass for mid-thirties.

'So.' She claps her perfectly manicured hands together on the table, turning to look at me. 'Charlotte, I want to know all about you!'

Oh god. She's someone that talks in exclamation points. Dread fills my veins. She is so. Damn. Cheerful.

'What do you want to know?' I ask, self-consciously tucking a bit of hair behind my ear. I should have at least curled it or something. Anything to make myself look even ten percent better next to this supermodel.

Luckily the waiter catches me a break by giving us our menus. I pretend to look it over when I already know what I'm having. I stalked the menu hard last night.

'Well first of all how did you two meet?' She looks to Arthur. 'Artie was so vague on the phone.

This Artie business is making me want to grab a bread knife and shove it into her chest. I'm not normally so stabby.

Arthur looks to me. Only a trained eye would see the split second of panic in his eyes. But she seems to know him *so* well so maybe she sees it too.

'You know how he can be.' She shrills a laugh, smiling at him as if he hung the moon.

Not really. I barely know the man.

'It was at the civil servants award,' I answer for him.

She frowns. 'Oh, so over a year ago?' She turns to Arthur. 'You are such a dark horse!'

He smiles tightly but doesn't correct her.

We place our orders and I start practically salivating at the thought of my garlic bread starter and rigatoni with aubergine and salted ricotta cheese, French fries on the side. Yummy.

'So where are you from?' she asks. Did she just side eye me slightly?

'From Watford, but my parents now live in Devon.'

In separate houses because they're lunatics who love to hate each other. But she doesn't need to know that.

'Oh how *lovely*. My parents have a summer place in Devon. So lovely down there. And I've heard Watford is very... *up and coming.*' She laughs as if that's hilarious.

I tense my jaw. Really? Insulting my hometown? What a bitch. Arthur hasn't noticed. Of course he hasn't. He's too busy checking his phone in between smiling back at James.

'I loved growing up in Watford,' I say proudly, puffing out my chest. 'I take it you're from London?'

'Oh no,' she giggles, which is *beyond* annoying. 'I grew up in the Kent countryside. I only moved to London after university.'

Shit, I've just realised I don't know where they actually went. I should probably know that about my fake fiancé.

'And Cambridge was never the same again,' Arthur chuckles, as if reliving a fond memory.

Shit, this guy is in love with her. He doesn't even realise it himself, but he is. He hasn't looked at me once like that. I'm just the silly bitch that got pregnant and trapped him. Damn. I feel so small right now.

And Cambridge? There's no way little old me can have a happily ever after with a dude that went to Cambridge. We're from different worlds.

She smiles back at him. 'We actually had dorm rooms next to each other. Then we decided to house share the years after that while we got our degrees and our masters.'

I nod, forcing interest. 'How lovely. What did you get your degree in?'

'I got my *masters*' she reiterates, 'in International Relations.'

'Oh wow.' I can't help but be impressed.

There was me hoping she was just a glamorous bimbo that got into university thanks to Daddy's donation.

'What about you?' She smiles encouragingly at me.

'Well, I just got a regular old degree,' I say with a self-conscious laugh. And there was me being pleased with my first.

She smiles sympathetically like I'm already an idiot not to have a masters. I'm dreading telling her and I just know she's going to push.

'Don't worry, that's fine.'

I know it is, bitch.

'So, what was it in?' She stares at me expectantly, her eyes feeling like they're penetrating my soul.

I look to Arthur who smiles encouragingly.

'It was in Fashion Design.' I try to say it with the same confidence she said, International Relations.

Her smile drops, but she quickly recovers. 'Oh how lovely! And are you a fashion designer now?'

Oh god. I'm going to sound so pathetic.

'Charlotte did work for the fashion house Blueberry,' Arthur says, kindly jumping in to help.

He smiles at me, as if to say, *I've got you*, and I need it more than he'll ever realise.

'But now she's working at Whitehall doing amazing work.'

'Oh marvellous.'

'What is it you do?' I ask quickly, eager to take the attention from me.

She pushes her glossy hair back from her face. 'I'm a diplomat. I've been stationed in Dubai for the last few years, but...' She looks to Arthur. 'I've decided that I'm moving back to London.'

His eyebrows raise. 'Really?'

Shit.

'Of course. I'm not going to miss baby Ellison being born!' She grabs my belly again and squeezes. Ugh. It takes everything in me not to push her off and slap her round the face.

'Well...' I say, looking to Arthur. 'We haven't actually discussed whether it's going to be baby Ellison or baby Bellswain Ellison.'

His face drops. 'I just assumed it would be Ellison?'

'Oh dear,' she says with an amused squirm. 'It seems you still have a few things to sort out before baby is born.'

Yeah thanks for the reminder, *James*. This girl might as well have got a masters in being passive aggressive.

Our starters arrive. Some funky smell is suddenly around us. I look to James' plate and she's ordered oysters. Normally fish doesn't bother me at all, but these are pretty strong smelling. They must have gone bad, surely? I try to ignore it and tuck into my garlic bread, but my stomach starts recoiling.

Keep it together Charlotte. Keep it together. It's just a bloody smell.

James starts telling a story about their university days while I try to reason with my own body. Is it hot in here? Its suddenly like I'm in a furnace, sweat prickling down my neck.

'Mmm,' James moans, cracking open another and letting it slide down her throat. 'Artie you *have* to try this!'

He leans in and lets her tip one into his mouth. Into. His. Mouth.

That's it. The last disgusting, inappropriate straw.

My stomach rolls and before I can run to the toilets, or even stand up, I'm throwing up into my garlic bread. I look up, vomit dripping down my chin to see Arthur and James looking back at me in wide eyed horror.

I pant, wiping my chin. Everyone in the restaurant has stopped to stare in a horrifying silence. My skin crawls from the humiliation. Please say this is a nightmare.

Arthur jumps up and passes me my glass of water. I take it and then proceed to throw up into that.

Oh my god. I have to get out of here. I'm behaving like that girl from the exorcist. Somebody call a priest!

I push my chair out, standing so abruptly I take the tablecloth with me, dragging my plate to the floor, clattering loudly around my feet.

'Ugh!' I scream in horror, my cheeks on fire. I turn and run the hell out of there as fast as I can.

14

Arthur

She runs from the restaurant without a coat. She'll be freezing out there. I go to follow her but James stops me, hand on my arm.

'Let her go, Art. She's obviously embarrassed.'

I sigh, everyone in the restaurant is staring, all I hope is none of them sell this story to the paper. It's the last thing she needs. Luckily they still haven't uncovered anything about her parents yet.

I call over a waiter. 'I'm so sorry about this. My fiancé is pregnant.'

He nods in understanding. 'It's no worry at all, sir.' He signals for another waiter to start cleaning it up.

'Actually, could I please have her main meal and a dessert to go?'

'Of course, sir.'

James touches my arm, a pout on her lips. 'Artie, don't go. I haven't seen you for months.'

This is just like James. Only thinking about herself. Don't get me wrong, I love her to bits, but she's always thinking of number one. It's why I could never fancy her.

'Yes, well the mother of my child is unwell, so I'll be going home to look after her.'

She follows me to get our coats while they cook the food. She continues pouting, deep in thought. I roll my eyes.

'Oh for God's sakes, James, just spit it out. It's all over your face.'

She sighs. 'I just... I don't see you two together. You seem polar opposites.'

I lean against the wall. 'Yes and they say opposites attract.'

She raises her eyebrows at me. 'They might attract but it doesn't mean they'll work.'

I check my phone, only to avoid her. She's been back two minutes and I'm already sick of her shit.

'Plus, they're saying you met at *this* year's civil servant awards. Not last year. Is that right?'

'Who is saying that?' I ask, with a pointed stare. I hate being the topic of gossip.

She rolls her eyes. 'Everyone.'

The waiter comes over with a bag of food. 'Thanks.'

I turn back to her. 'Well, luckily for me I don't give a shit what everyone thinks.'

Charlotte

I get in and throw my purse onto the sofa. That couldn't have possibly gone worse. The sad part is that now I've been sick I'm bloody starving again. I look in the fridge and all that's in there is healthy food. Lots of those chicken and vegetables meals he gets delivered. Ugh. Gross. I want carbs and cheese.

I turn the TV on and settle down in front of it with my make up remover. As I start stripping my face I relive the horror of earlier, physically cringing whenever I think about it. What a first impression.

God, how can he be friends with someone so bitchy? It's just another reminder that I'm not part of his world. She works as a diplomat for God's sake. She was born to be with him. Not that she's diplomatic when she's slagging off my hometown or fashion degree.

And look how he didn't run after me. It took me ages to get a cab and he still wasn't out of there. I can't pretend it doesn't sting. I need to start thinking if I really want this. Do I want to feel second best for the rest of my life? Like I'm always so much less than him? Not that he's said he'll actually marry me. I have no idea when he sees this ending.

I want my baby to have a family, but I don't want to resign myself to a life of misery where I end up resenting him. I grew up in a toxic environment and don't want that for my child.

My make up is off when the door rattles and I automatically glance up to see him walking in.

I quickly turn away. I don't think I can look at him right now. I'd likely either growl or burst into tears.

'Hey,' he says.

'Hi,' I answer curtly, eyes not moving from the TV.

He grabs something from the cupboard and then walks in front of me. He empties a bag and I see that he's brought my dinner back for me.

My mouth drops open at the kind gesture.

'You brought me food?' I utter in surprise, all anger dissipating.

He nods, placing a knife and fork down for me. Wow. Just when I'm sure he's a heartless bastard he does something sweet.

I waste no time tucking in. Oh my god it's amazing. Still warm.

'How are you feeling?'

I look up to see his forehead puckered with lines. He's genuinely concerned. *For the baby* I remind myself.

'Better now.' I squirm, thinking about it again. 'Sorry to have embarrassed you.'

He sits down next to me, loosening his tie. 'You didn't embarrass me. I was just worried about you.'

I snort. 'Is that why you didn't come running after me?'

Ugh, why did I say that? I just sound like a catty bitch. He hasn't made me any promises.

He frowns. 'I just thought you'd be sad to miss out on the food.'

I mean, he's right, but it's annoying that he is. I still would have liked him to have ran out onto the street after me. Is that too much to ask?

'I'm sorry I ruined your night with James.'

I can't stop thinking about her judging tone. How he didn't realise she was belittling me. And now she's moving here.

He grabs my chin and turns my face so that I have to look up into his dark brown eyes, finding them filled with warmth and kindness.

'You didn't ruin anything. You and this baby have made my life.'

My mouth drops open. Oh my god. Did he really just say that? Swoon!

I look down at his lips, desperate to kiss him. Desperate for him to want to kiss me. To tangle our bodies and forget this highly complicated situation we've found ourselves in. Too soon he pulls back and stands up.

'Goodnight, Charlotte.'

'Goodnight.'

I open up the dessert box, eager to find out what he ordered for me. He didn't know what I'd selected. Toffee cheesecake. Damn. That's what I planned to order.

How is it I've met my dream man but we've been doomed from the beginning?

Friday 23rd October

Charlotte

I've decided not to dwell on James moving back here. I can't control that. I'm going to busy myself with something I can control, getting excited for the baby's nursery. After work I find a tape measure in his drawer, grab a paper and pen and head to the baby's room.

I'm so excited, my stomach bubbling while my mind spins with potential ideas. I'm going to start a Pinterest board first for inspiration. Then I can't wait to whittle it down to a theme, look for furniture, check out all of the safety reviews. I'll do a spreadsheet in order of price. Organising is my thing. I actually enjoy it. One of the reasons I'm stuck being an assistant to people more important than me.

I open the door but halt in my tracks when I see the room already decorated. I'm so confused I actually lean back out and check I'm in the right apartment. I'm not imagining things, right?

No, this is our place. Only someone has snuck in and

totally transformed the room. No longer is it set up as an office, instead the walls have been painted white with a plush white carpet fitted. Modern white and black furniture already fill the room. I walk over to the cot and look at the black and white sheep mobile, reaching in and feeling the black blanket.

The room stinks of that overpowering perfume I smelt the other day. At least I know he's not shagging around I suppose.

Why the hell would he do this? Get the nursery decorated without consulting me first? And in black and fucking white of all colours. It's a fine bedroom... if you're Wednesday fucking Adams.

More than my hate for the colour, and general theme of choice, is the devastation that this has been robbed from me. I wanted to do my own baby's nursery. Is that really too much to ask?

Before I know it I'm crying. Not just because of the nursery, but because it's just another reminder that this is so far removed from what I imagined me having my first baby would be. I just assumed I'd be happily married to the man of my dreams. We'd be settled in some house in Watford and we'd spend our weekends at baby stores and B&Q, doing everything ourselves. I'd tell the baby how Mummy and Daddy decorated everything by hand, poured all of our love into making their room perfect. I wouldn't be saying that its father went behind my back and paid some interior fucking decorator to do it all.

'Ah, you've seen it.'

I turn to see Arthur has come in. He smiles, as if expecting me to thank him, to be over the moon that he stole my privilege to do it.

I quickly turn and wipe away the tears forming in my

eyes. It's too close to the restaurant vomiting incident to be causing a scene again. Especially when I'm sure he thinks he's done a nice thing.

'Yeah,' I offer lamely, plastering a fake smile onto my lips.

He rubs his forehead. 'I thought you'd be pleased.'

God, this stranger doesn't know me at all.

'Thought it would take a worry off your mind.'

'Mmm.' It's almost impossible for me to lie to his face. It's easier to just smile and be vague.

His face drops in realisation. 'Oh no. You hate it don't you?'

How the hell can he tell? I'm grinning like a Cheshire Cat. Maybe I'm more grimacing?

'No, no, it's great,' I insist. I even sound unconvincing, my voice flat.

'Not your style?' He walks closer to me and has a look in the cot. 'I suppose it is quite a strong look. I just told her we wanted something gender neutral. And I've read babies can only see black and white in the first few months.'

It's sweet that he's done some baby research.

He turns to look at me, lifting my chin so I'm forced to look into his deep dark eyes.

'Just be honest with me,' he commands, his voice quiet, filled with sincerity.

I sigh. Now or never I suppose. If I don't speak up now I'll be raising a goth child. Not that me and Eloise didn't go through that stage ourselves. I hope to God no one ever unearths those pictures.

'It's not just the design. It's that I was looking forward to us doing it ourselves.'

He frowns. 'Oh. I just... I'm always working. I thought this would be easier.'

He's not interested in other words.

'And it is,' I say with a nod. 'But easier doesn't always mean better.'

His lips turn half-heartedly. 'You're right. I'm sorry, I should have checked with you. Just scrap it and start again. We can do it however you like.'

I smile, even though that's not what I wanted to hear. I wanted him to tell me he's interested and that we can plan it together. Drive to Ikea and get the furniture, argue over putting it together. Just normal couple stuff regular people take for granted. But I'm quickly realising that nothing with Arthur Ellison is going to be regular.

15

Monday 26th October

Arthur

I can't believe I fucked up so royally with the nursery. Charlotte keeps surprising me. Every other woman I've ever known would have loved a well-known interior decorator to do their decorating. They'd probably have tried to book an OK magazine shoot so they could brag about it.

But with Charlotte all bets are off. I can't seem to put a foot right recently. I know she's extra hormonal with the baby, but I feel like I'm walking on eggshells.

I'm just about to prepare for my next meeting when James calls.

'Morning, James.'

'Hey Artie, how are you?'

I'm still pissed off with how rude she was about Charlotte the other night.

'Fine thank you,' I answer curtly. 'And you?'

'Oh please stop being upset with me.' I can imagine her pouting. 'I'm sorry about the other night. I was jet lagged and extra bitchy. Forgive me?'

I've never been able to stay mad at her long.

'Fine, but only if you put in more of an effort with Charlotte. She's important to me.'

'I will, I promise.'

'Good.'

'I actually bumped into Victoria. She was telling me she designed the nursery. She showed me some pictures and wow! It's so chic. I can't wait to see it.'

She's trying to get herself invited round. It's not just my apartment anymore so I don't.

'Well, we're not exactly keeping that design.'

'Why?'

'Well, Charlotte didn't exactly love it.' It's hard to say it without her coming across as a spoilt princess.

'Really? Why not?'

'Err... I think she wanted more colour. Plus, she's been looking forward to designing it herself.'

'Ah, I suppose it's the creative soul in her. Well tell her I'm around if she needs any help.'

I roll my eyes. Yeah, as if Charlotte would want her help.

'That's really sweet of you. Thank you.'

'Lunch next week?'

I hesitate. If I have the time I'd rather take Charlotte out.

'If I have time, yes.'

'Oh and I'm helping your mum plan her Christmas Eve party. Remember to tell Charlotte to put it in her diary.'

'Will do.'

Wednesday 28th October

Charlotte – 28 Weeks Pregnant

I'm drafting a memo Roger's asked me to sort out when that sick feeling creeps into my stomach again. Oh god, not now. I don't have time to feel rough, there's too much to do.

My temperature soars and within seconds I know it's coming. I stand, attempting to run to the toilets but it's clear this vomit is not waiting for anyone. I search around in a panic. Where's the bin? Why isn't it under my desk? In my hysteria I choose the plant behind my desk. It's not much, but as soon as it leaves my stomach I feel instantly better. I look around to see if anyone noticed but luckily my desk is away from others.

I just need to clean this plant up before the smell creeps up and I vomit again. I stand and, as discreetly as possible lift it up, still in its pot and carry it towards the toilet. It's a big heavy bastard and it's hard in these red stilettos, but I wasn't exactly expecting an active day when I got dressed this morning. That and the leopard print heel matches my new maternity dress perfectly. I felt so chic when I left the flat. Now I'm huffing and puffing like I'm going to blow the little pigs house down. I'm getting so out of breath doing the most basic stuff nowadays.

'Charlotte?' Edward, a man in his sixties with red braces, says, passing me in the hall. 'What are you doing with that plant?' He looks down his spectacles at me.

'Oh, just... taking it to be watered.'

He scowls back at me. 'Surely it would be easier to bring a jug of water to the plant?'

Of course that's would be easier. I'll have to play dumb. I

hate having to play stupid. I feel like I let down every female I know.

'Oh yes! Silly me! What am I like?' I fake a laugh, my cheeks heating with embarrassment.

I should have the right to vote taken away from me. I'm a disgrace.

I turn and hurry quickly down the hallway to the bathroom. I take it out of its pot and run the tap, attempting to remove my own vomit from the earth. Ugh, and now I'm heaving again. This is a disaster, muddy soil going everywhere.

I try to wash it from my hands, while heaving into another sink. I hear something clink against the porcelain. I look down to see my engagement ring has slipped off my finger and is circling the drain.

No! I watch helplessly as it slips down just before I can grab it. Shit!

I try to look down the plughole, but I can't see it. Fuck a duck. Arthur's priceless heirloom. The ring his Grandma told him to give to the woman he marries. And this dickhead has only gone and lost it. Crap!

My heart starts beating so fast I can hear it thrashing in my ears. I open the cupboard under the sink and look at the tubes. Surely I can loosen them myself? I struggle but get nowhere. Crap I'm gonna have to call a plumber. But then they won't let anyone in unless they're on the cleared list.

I run back to my desk and grab my phone. Then I go back to the bathroom and call down to Pat on reception.

'Pat, we need an urgent plumber. Do you have anyone on the books?'

'We do, why? What's happened?'

'Oh it's...' I can hardly tell her the truth. 'Um, I've got a... something... that I can't flush and its flooding.'

'Oh Jesus. Okay I'll call them now.'

Now every time Pat looks at me she'll be imagining a giant floater.

I can't risk leaving this sink for someone to flush it further into the system, potentially never to be seen again. Just the idea of it is giving me palpitations.

So I wait the excruciating hour and a half for the plumber to arrive. Then I grovel and tell him the truth, hoping he'll take pity on a pregnant woman.

'You're that bird that was on the telly. Aren't you engaged to the Cabinet Secretary?'

I grimace. 'Yep. And if we don't find my ring I'm going to be in a mountain of shit.'

He chuckles. 'Don't worry, love, I'll sort it for you.'

He eventually retrieves the ring, thank God! After thanking him and promising to call my baby after him (Geoff, no chance) I rush back to my desk, hoping no one has noticed my two hour absence.

'Charlotte!' Roger calls when he spots me. 'My office. NOW.'

No such luck.

Arthur

I walk by her desk at the end of work, wondering if she'll still be here. Low and behold she is, typing away at her computer. Her eyes are not only rimmed with heavy purple bags but they're also pink. Has she been crying?

'Charlotte. Are you okay?'

She looks up, her chin wobbly. 'Yeah.'

I can tell it's taking all of her strength to even say that.

'Are you sure? You look exhausted.' I push some hair back from her face without thinking.

I want to gather her in my arms and take away all her problems.

'Please,' she begs, looking up at me with those gorgeous hazel eyes. 'Just let me finish.'

I look at my watch. 'It's half past bloody eight. I'm not having this.'

I walk into Roger's office. He's on his iPhone, no doubt fucking around playing Candy Crush. The lazy fuck.

'Roger, can you please tell me why Charlotte is still out there working at this time?'

He rolls his eyes. 'Maybe if she wouldn't have gone missing for two hours earlier she'd have finished all her work.'

That's weird.

'Where was she?'

'Stomach problems, apparently.'

Shit, I hope she's okay.

'Whatever, I'm taking her home.'

'Throwing your weight around now she's your pregnant fiancé, are you?' he dares ask.

I scoff back at him. 'Remember who you're talking to Roger. I'm your superior. I bet HR would like to hear about you making a pregnant woman work late.'

He screws his face up. 'Oh fuck off, Arthur. Don't pretend you gave a shit when my wife was expecting and you were constantly riding my arse every night for reports.'

Shit, I suppose I did do that. This pregnancy is making me realise what an arsehole I've been.

'Regardless. I'm taking her home.'

I walk out and nod at her. 'Get your coat. We're leaving.'

Charlotte

'Thanks for getting me out of there,' I say as soon as we're home, sitting down on the sofa.

My butt has never been so grateful for a comfy seat. Roger already hated me. Going missing only fuelled the fire.

'Why were you missing for two hours?'

Oh god, Roger told him.

'Um... I was sick.' I take off my shoes. They may be stunning but I don't see myself wearing them again until after the pregnancy.

He frowns. 'Should we be concerned you're getting sick in the second trimester? Is that normal?'

I shrug. 'Who knows. I don't think there's anything normal about this pregnancy.'

He grins and leans down to my stomach. 'That's because you're growing our super baby.' He cups my stomach affectionately, smiling up at me.

It's the most affectionate thing he's ever done. As if realising this he straightens up, clears his throat and walks to the kitchen. 'Oh, do you have plans for Christmas Eve?' he calls back.

I shrug. 'Not sure. Oh, but while I remember Eloise is having a Halloween party this weekend and has invited us.'

'Both of us?' he asks, chewing on his lip.

'Yep. You don't have to come if you don't fancy it, but it'll be nice for me to see some old friends.'

He nods, as if mulling it over. 'Okay. I'd like to meet your friends.'

It's worrying how happy that makes me.

'Great. What's happening Christmas Eve?'

'My mum's annual Christmas Eve party.'

My stomach drops. Damn it. Now I have to go to that

pompous party and enter into Christmas heavily pregnant surrounded by pompous toffs.

'Can't wait.'

Saturday 31st October

Arthur

Eloise's Halloween party isn't going to be my scene but I said yes immediately. I want to be a part of her life and more than that I want her to feel comfortable with me mingling with her friends. It's in my best interests to get to know these people. After all they will be hanging around with my baby in the future no doubt.

She looks absolutely adorable dressed as a pumpkin. She already had an orange dress, so she's stitched on a pumpkin face to where the bump sits and teamed it with black and white striped tights, ankle boots and a green hairband that acts as the pumpkin sprout.

'You sure you're ready for this?' she asks as we knock on the door of the Watford flat.

I grin. She's so cute when she's nervous. 'Too late now.'

I take her hand in mine and give it a squeeze. She looks down at it with a frown. Oh god, maybe she doesn't want me touching her like this. There's so many blurred lines between us.

Eloise swings the door open to her ground floor flat. She's dressed as a devil, wearing only a red swimming suit with matching tights, thigh high boots and devil horns. Jesus Christ. I knew she had a fiery side but I've never seen her in anything but work wear.

'You're here!' she exclaims, seemingly already half cut. 'Come in.'

She grabs Charlotte and drags her in. Her hand drops out of mine and I follow behind feeling like a sheep going to the slaughter.

The whole place is in darkness apart from pumpkin LED lights which are draped amongst crime tape. Well, she definitely went to town. Not that Charlotte didn't warn me. She said last year they got complaints from the neighbours because their window display was too terrifying for children.

I follow them down a narrow hallway already crowded with people clutching drinks chatting and into the back kitchen. It's a small box room with an old-fashioned kitchen last decorated sometime in the eighties.

Despite the size I count fifteen people squeezed into it. Some are mixing drinks, others sat on the counter eating Pringles from the tin and laughing. When they spot Charlotte they all stop what they're doing and rush to coo over her bump, tell her how cute she is and how they haven't seen her for ages. I stand back, feeling like a spare part.

Maybe I should have just let her come on her own. Maybe she only invited me to be polite and didn't actually want me here.

She turns to me, as they still fuss all over her. God, she's gorgeous. I don't think I'll ever tire of looking at her. The best part is she seems completely unaware of it. She smiles self-consciously and puts her hand out for me to take. I step closer and take it, thankful for the lifeline.

'And this is Arthur.'

'Dang!' her mixed-race friend with the braids says, 'I heard he was yummy, but I didn't realise how much of a snack!'

Err… is it good to be referred to as a snack?

Eloise and Charlotte start laughing so I grin along feeling like an idiot. Is this how the kids are speaking nowadays? I feel like a dinosaur.

'Thank you?' I offer, cringing.

'So you're the guy that got our Char knocked up,' another with pink hair says with a cheeky grin.

'Hey, he put a ring on it,' another with long blonde hair says, giving me a kind nod.

'I did indeed.' Before I have time to reason with myself, I lift our entwined fingers and kiss the back of her hand.

They all coo with *'ahs'*. Charlotte goes bright red. I love how it's almost impossible for her to hide her embarrassment. I just don't know if she's embarrassed to be associated with me or if it's from me showing affection.

A black guy hands me a bottle of Peroni. 'I think you're going to need this being around this lot.' He smiles and its clear in an instant he's another suffering spouse.

I smile back, glad for the comradery. Looks like I am going to need it. Long night ahead of me.

16

Charlotte

I can't believe how well Arthur is getting on with everyone. I mean, of course when we first arrived he looked like he wanted to run in the opposite direction. Especially when Eloise greeted us dressed as a devil slut, but now he's chatting to the gang like he's known them for years. They've told him all of my cringe worthy stories from back when I was a teenager and he's laughed along. I know I'm going to get mercilessly ribbed about it later.

Well that's if he remembers, he's had quite a lot to drink. Me being sober I've noticed it more, how his shoulders have relaxed, his smile appearing easier. He's so adorable like this. This guy I could fall in love with. The '*Time Warp*' comes blasting out of the speakers.

'Oh my god, I love this song!' I grab him by the shoulders. 'Come on!'

I drag him into the sitting room which is the makeshift dance floor. I start doing the dance, but he doesn't seem to know it, his panicked eyes darting over my moves. Who the hell doesn't know the '*Time Warp*'? I'd want my money back from that boarding school.

He copies all of us and before we know it he's doing it to perfection, shaking his shoulders and hips. I've never seen him so loose and happy.

When I look at him right now I'm over the moon he somehow became my baby daddy. I don't think there's a better man out there for the job.

We call a cab soon after as I can tell he's going to be feeling it in the morning. He cuddles up to me in the back of the black cab, allowing his gorgeous scent to invade my nostrils. God, he smells delicious.

'You had a good time then?' I ask, grinning back at his sleepy smile. His curls are spilling around his eyes.

'I had the best time. You're great, you know that? You're so great.'

He leans forward and kisses me on the lips. It's so fleeting I'm not even one hundred percent sure it happened. He rests his head against my shoulder and is asleep in seconds. What the hell did that mean? Or did it mean nothing?

The cab driver helps me bring him in, he's such a big bastard. I tip him well and start removing his clothes so that he doesn't suffocate.

'Ooh, cheeky wife to be!' he chuckles, still half asleep.

'I'm just trying to make sure you don't choke in your sleep,' I answer, fully out of breath from the exertion of trying to help him.

He squishes his face against the pillow, his eyes shut. 'You're going to make such a good wife.'

I freeze. Wife? That's the second time he's said that word. We never talked about *actually* getting married. This is supposed to be a fake engagement purely for show. But then he did kiss me in the cab. Is he having mixed feelings? They say the truth comes out when you're drunk.

God, why are we always so messy? I strip out of my dress and lie down next to him, knowing I'll be tossing and turning all night over-analysing everything.

Sunday 1st November

Charlotte

When I wake I'm alone and its already nearly midday. Wow I slept like a log. All of that worrying must have exhausted me. I wander into the living room to see Arthur just coming in all sweaty from a run. How the hell can he be exercising the day after a session? Is it weird I want to lick the sweat from him? *Yes, Charlotte, it is.*

'Hey, how are you feeling?' I ask, self-consciously busying myself by playing with the coffee machine. I wonder if he remembers last night.

'Ugh, better now,' he chuckles, still out of breath. 'I can't believe how much I put away last night. I felt rough this morning.'

'I bet.' I push my wayward hair down. He still manages to look delectable. 'I actually feel exhausted and I didn't even drink.'

'It'll be all that dancing.' He winks and my heart flip flops.

Okay so he remembers the dancing. I suppose you don't forget you learnt the '*Time Warp*'. I was twelve at my auntie's New Year's Eve party.

'I'm just gonna have a shower and then I was thinking we could go shopping for nursery bits?'

Oh my god. And now he wants to buy baby stuff? Has he morphed into my dream man overnight? I need to get him drunk more often.

'Okay. That sounds great.'

TWO HOURS later we're in a baby shop at Westfields shopping centre. I need to somehow also buy breast pads today. I know it's stupid to not want him to know that my boobs have started to leak, but well, it's weird. *I* still haven't come to terms with it and it's my body.

'I like this,' I say, feeling the fleecy blanket of a woodland theme.

He scrunches his face up. 'I don't.'

'Why not?' There I was thinking he wouldn't care and he's gone the complete other way and become a fussy bastard. What's not to like about a woodland theme?

He pouts. 'What are we trying to achieve with a woodland theme? Do we want them to think they're sleeping in the woods? Or are you hoping they become a landscaper?'

I grit my teeth. 'I just thought it was charming. You know there is such a thing as over thinking.'

He rolls his eyes.

'What about this one?' I point to a grey cloud blanket. There's a yellow star pillow attached to it with *'dream big little one'* written on it. It's adorable.

He raises one eyebrow. 'So we're encouraging them to put their head in the clouds and daydream?'

'Jesus,' I snap, my jaw tensing. 'Then what about this? A nautical theme?'

'Hello sailor,' he jokes in a camp voice.

'Ugh, you are impossible!' I storm off needing some space between us. We're never going to agree to anything at this rate. Where's the guy that was happy with the Wednesday Adams nursery?

I wander over to the buggies. Hmm, this one is nice. Black with rose gold handles, chic without being showy.

'I like this one,' he says appearing at my side.

My mouth nearly touches the floor. Are we actually agreeing on something? Praise the Lord!

I check the price tag. Shit the bed. Nearly a grand and a half for the entire travel system.

'Er, let's look at the ones over there.'

I go to move but he takes my arm, stopping me. I look up to see him studying my face. 'Why are you being weird?'

'No reason.' My voice sounds high and screechy. Way to act weird.

He keeps hold of me while the other hand reaches for the price tag. He checks it and seems completely unshocked.

'Is it because of the price?' He narrows his eyes, his lips pursed.

See rich people drop that kind of money all the time and don't even think about it. I might be on slightly more money than my old job and he might be insisting I don't pay any rent, but I still don't want to pay that kind of money. It's just a buggy. Hell, my first car cost that much.

'I just think we can get something more reasonable.'

He rubs his forehead. 'Why?'

I sigh. I don't have the energy for a fight, but I want to be clear about this.

'Because I want to pay half.' I brace for impact. I know this isn't going to go down well.

He drops my arm, obviously blindsided.

'Charlotte, don't be ridiculous.' He shakes his head in disbelief. 'I make more money, it only makes sense that I'll pay for it.'

Typical rich person, throwing his money around.

'It's my baby too, so it only makes sense that we go halves.'

'Halfsies?' He mocks, one eyebrow raised, the ghost of a smile on the edge of his mouth. 'You're being ridiculous.'

Hot anger surges through my body. I despise when he calls me ridiculous. It makes me feel like some silly little girl that can't be trusted to make a decision.

Take a deep breath, Charlotte. Now is not the place to murder him. Far too many witnesses. I've watched enough true crime to know how to do it right.

'I'm just being practical. You're the one always talking about being a team. This is how being a team works.'

He flattens his lips. 'You're just being stubborn. There really is no need.' He steps closer, completely into my space. So close I can small his minty breath mingled with his aftershave. It's unfair. He knows his scent makes me silly. He tucks a strand of hair behind my ear, causing goosebumps to rise on my arms.

'When are you going to realise that I'm here to take care of you?'

My stomach trembles with fear. Fear of relenting and letting myself rely on him, only to be let down and left high and dry. The thought makes my stomach churn. I don't want to set myself up for disappointment. I'm better off relying on myself, always have been. Even my own parents have let me down multiple times.

Only... hang on a minute. I don't think my trembly tummy is all down to my feelings. I think my stomach is in trouble. It rolls again, making an audible sound. Oh my god.

Right on cue I release a fart. A silent but deadly fart.

My eyes widen the second I smell it. I thought it would stay in the fake leather maternity leggings longer, sadly not. They're so tight I imagine them inflating instead.

I grab Arthur and drag him away. I have turned into a treacherous beast of a woman and he is never to know.

'Come on. I want to look at these buggies over there.'

He stiffens his posture, head held high defiantly. 'I've already told you, cost is not a problem.'

'No, come on!' I beg, trying to communicate with my eyes that we need to escape. 'I mean it.'

I'm sweating now. This cute peach jumper is doing nothing to help the situation. The minute he sniffs it the will be game over. He'll never be able to fancy me or maybe even look at me again.

'You need to stop being so—' he pauses.

Oh no. He's smelt it. My eyes widen in horror. It's the beginning of the end.

'Ugh, what is that smell?' He starts coughing. Shit, it's so potent it's going to kill him.

I have no other choice. I turn and run before anyone else has a chance to smell it. Out of the shop and away from the nuclear gas that came out of my arse. I'm sure someone will run to his aid if he *is* dying. People don't ignore sexy people struggling.

My stomach churns again, only this time I know I need the actual toilet. Shit. Literally.

I search around frantically for a sign of the toilets. I need to get there, like yesterday. I can't see a sign. Dammit, this is my first time to Westfields. I normally shop online or at

Brent Cross. I don't have my bearings and I'm breaking in new grey ankle boots. What the hell was I thinking?

'Charlotte?' Arthur's here again having followed me out. Okay, so he's not dead. 'Was that you?' he whispers.

Jesus, is he trying to kill me with humiliation?

'Where are the toilets?' I shout, already deciding on a direction and running towards it. 'Where are the toilets?' I shout at passers-by minding their own business. They stare back with wide eyes, obviously thinking I'm crazy.

One woman finally points, someone taking pity. 'They're at the end, love.'

Of fucking course they are. I start running, but it's like every leap I take just has my arse trying to expel it. I power walk instead, but it's just as bad. Sweat is running down my neck from the stress of trying to hold it in. There is literally no way I am going to be able to make it in time.

Please God, I pray. I'll do anything. Just don't have me shit myself in public. I've gone thirty-one years without this level of humiliation, I don't want to start now. Not when I'm with Arthur.

The sweat is pouring off my forehead. Arthur keeps running to keep up with me. He needs to fuck off. He cannot witness this.

'Leave me alone!' I shout with barred teeth.

'I don't understand. What did I do?' he asks, blinking rapidly.

'This isn't about you,' I growl.

Oh god, now I feel nauseous too, sick creeping up my oesophagus. If I vomit at the same time as shitting I will die. *Actually* die.

Dying would be easier than this, surely.

I see it! I see the toilet sign. It's within sight. I've never been so pleased to see that little woman in a dress sign.

Don't shit yourself now, Charlotte. You're so near the end. The win is within sight.

Arthur is still running after me, asking me all kinds of questions, but I can't even look at him right now, let alone listen to him. I need to focus on just this one task: not pooing my pants.

I'm here. Halleluiah. I'm at the toilets. I run through the door but all that greets me is the longest hallway in the world. I'm doomed.

I sprint down it, already tugging at the elastic of my legging. It's happening. It's starting to happen. I have no control over it. I'm losing my fucking mind.

'Charlotte!' Arthur shouts at me, his voice echoing down the corridor.

'I'm going to shit!' I scream back, all self-respect long gone out the window.

I slam the toilet door open, rip the leggings down my thighs and sit on the toilet before even shutting the door.

I have the most severe shits I've ever experienced. What the hell has happened to me? The most terrifying noises shudder out of me. Growls I wouldn't expect from an animal, let alone a human.

I rip my jumper off over my head, feeling like I'm suffocating.

When it's finally over I realise that I did in fact shit myself, my knickers and leggings ruined. I'm sat in just my bra, still too hot to attempt the jumper. There is no way I can just pull these leggings up and run to the car. Ugh, fuck my life.

What the hell am I going to do? I need Arthur's help. This is where I kiss goodbye to ever being able to look him in the eye again. It's my only hope though. I need to get home somehow.

Eloise is back in Watford so there's no way she could get here. Oh god, what has my life come to? I'm a disaster.

I get my phone out and write out a text to him.

I need you to please go and buy me a new pair of maternity jeans/leggings and a loose t-shirt. Bring it into the toilet and leave it by the sink with a packet of baby wipes. I also need you to never speak of this again.

There goes any self-respect I've been clinging onto.

17

Tuesday 3rd November

Charlotte – 29 Weeks Pregnant

*T*rue to his word, we didn't speak of it. He brought me my new jeans and a t-shirt and then we drove straight home in silence. Looking back, I think the non-alcoholic drink I'd purchased for Eloise's Halloween party mustn't have agreed with me. It was sugar free and Eloise reckons they put sweeteners in it instead which if you take too many can act as a laxative. She's the perfect person to be around *after* an emergency.

'Charlotte.'

I look up to see James standing in front of my desk.

'James,' I say completely dumbfounded. I must look like such an idiot. I hate being caught off guard. 'What are you doing here?'

She smiles, but I see her eyes sweep over my outfit in

judgement. There I was thinking I looked good today in my black shift dress with white pussy bow collar. She looks a million miles better in a simple black polo neck paired with a double layered mesh midi skirt in caramel with black posies adorning it.

'I thought I'd take you out for lunch.'

'Oh... okay.' I look at the clock and its bang on lunch time. I search around my mind for an excuse but can't think of one. Instead I stare back like a rabbit in headlights. Damn that baby brain.

Roger walks out of his office and spots her, his face lighting up like a Christmas tree. 'Ah, James. How the devil are you?'

Of *course* they know each other. Probably from the same aggressive polo club.

They air kiss like long lost friends. I'll have to pick her brain on how she knows him. He's such an arsehole; she must have some dirt on him.

'I'm taking Charlotte out, if alright with you?' She flutters her eyelashes and he's putty in her hands.

'Of course,' he says as if he's the most reasonable boss around. He turns to me. 'Charlotte, I've been meaning to ask you, do you know why that plant is dying?'

'The plant?' I repeat, playing for time.

I stare at it, its leaves limp and sad. I know exactly what plant he's talking about. The one I threw up in. I've tried watering it but it's like it's given up on life after the traumatic incident.

'Yes, this one.' He narrows his eyes at me. 'Have you been watering it?'

'Yes,' I nod, standing and getting my coat. 'How strange. Anyway I'll be back soon. Bye.'

'So,' James says excitedly as soon as we're sat down at far too a fancy restaurant for a quick lunch. I have three sets of cutlery. 'I have a surprise for you.'

I gulp, my stomach unsettled. 'You do?'

Shit. She's moving in, isn't she?

'I do.' She practically beams back at me, jumping in her seat. 'I've decided... that I'm going to throw your baby shower.'

My face drops along with my stomach. She wants to what?

'My baby shower?' I repeat back in disbelief. She can't be serious.

She nods, eyes glowing. 'I know how stressed you've been lately.'

Why does she think that? Has Arthur been telling her stuff? God, if he told her I shit myself I will leave him and never look back until I'm in Canada starting a new life.

'So I just thought I'd take this one thing from your shoulders. One less thing to worry about.'

'Oh, but...' how do I get out of this? 'I just assumed my best friend Eloise would plan it.'

You know, the girl that actually knows me.

She narrows her eyes. 'Well, has she offered?' She smirks, as if she already knows she hasn't.

'Well, no,' I begrudgingly admit, 'but I'm sure that's just because she's been very busy.'

'Well even better for me to take it off her busy hands then.' She smiles, her blue eyes insistent.

'Um... I'm sure she'd want to be the one to do it,' I press, avoiding her threatening eyes. 'She has after all been my best friend since we were teenagers.'

She shrugs. 'Well if she wants some input just give her my number. I'm happy for all hands-on deck.'

She's really not going to give in. I'm being bullied into it, whether I like it or not.

'Um... okay.'

It's easier to just go with it. A lifetime of being a referee between my parents has showed me arguing doesn't get you anywhere. Especially with someone so stubborn.

'Marvellous.' She claps her hands together as if it's a done deal. 'Now, let's talk themes.'

I groan. 'Me and Arthur can't even agree on a theme for the nursery, let alone a baby shower.'

I instantly regret telling her. I don't want her to run back to Arthur and say I've been slagging him off.

'Well,' she grins evilly, 'luckily for us the baby shower is nothing to do with him.'

I suppose she's right. And why shouldn't I be spoilt a little before my life is over for good? I need to look at this positively.

'So.' She reaches in her huge Michael Kors handbag, that I know costs just over four hundred pounds, and picks out a folder. 'I've whittled the themes down to three. Have a look at my mood boards and let me know which one you prefer.'

She hands it over. Why doesn't she just have a Pinterest board like everyone else?

I scan over the sheets of paper. She has put a hell of a lot of thought into it. I almost feel bad for wishing she wouldn't do it.

I can choose between Moon and Stars, Mum to Bee and Santa Baby. Each theme is more elaborate than the last.

'So?' she asks, eyes alight with excitement.

'Oh, you want a decision right now?'

She nods eagerly. 'I have to send the invitations out right away.'

'Right away. Why? When is it going to happen?' *And shouldn't I have some say in it?*

'Well,' she purses her lips, 'with Christmas and New Year being in the way, along with birthdays, etc the best date is Saturday 5th December.'

'Oh, okay.' Now the Santa Baby theme makes more sense. 'It's just a lot to think about.'

'That's why I'm here to make it easier.' She smiles keenly. 'I don't start my new job until the New Year so I have plenty of time to spare.'

Ah, so that's why she's so eager. And she really is trying to be my friend. I should make an effort, for Arthur's sake.

'Can I make a suggestion?' She leans in. 'What with Linda's Christmas eve party, I think discount that theme. Go for Moons and Stars. It'll be magical.'

Maybe I should do the same theme for the nursery. Arthur would probably be pleased thinking our child would grow up to be an astronomer.

'Okay. Looks like its Moons and Stars.'

She squeals in joy, clapping her hands together. 'You will not regret this. It's going to be epic!'

Then why do I already?

Thursday 5th November

Charlotte

Arthur is taking me out to dinner tonight. He said to make up for our disastrous dinner with James. He seemed pleased when I said I'd gone to lunch with her and that she was planning the baby shower. The cynical side of me wondered if the real reason James's doing it is to look amazing to Arthur. Or *Artie* as she calls him.

I just bloody hope to God I'm not sick again tonight. He said he's reserved a table far away from the kitchen and everyone else. He's also promised not to order any fish.

Even though I'm still exhausted from Roger being a demanding diva I'm looking forward to it. It weirdly feels like our first date. I have a long bath, shave practically my entire body (which is hard because I can no longer see the tops of my legs) while cursing being a female, and then blow dry my hair to perfection. I put my tongs in it to create a little wave at the ends. Then I apply my make up. Smoky eyes and a nude lip.

It's the first time in a long while that I actually feel pretty good about my appearance. The wine coloured floral midi dress I ordered looks good, I'm even getting used to the squelchy breast pads in my bra.

I know it's not a date and that we're not even together, but when he said that me and the baby had made his life, well it was hard not to swoon. He probably hasn't thought about it since, whereas I've replayed it in my head constantly and there's no denying I'm looking forward to going out with him.

I can feel myself falling for him harder each day. In a way I wish he were a bastard so I wouldn't have to risk being hurt. I already feel vulnerable enough and that's without indulging my heart in fantasies.

My phone rings, Arthur's name flashing up on the screen. My stomach tingles with excitement.

'Hi,' I sing cheerily down the phone.

'Hi.' He sighs.

I know that sigh. My stomach drops. It's bad news.

'I'm so sorry but I'm going to have to cancel dinner.'

'Oh.' It's hard to hide the disappointment. I mean, I put so much effort into getting all glammed up. Why couldn't he have cancelled earlier? I could be in my pjs by now.

'Yeah, we've got a last-minute meeting that we need to have, it looks like it's going to be a long one. I'm so sorry, Charlotte.'

'It's okay.' I try to sound more upbeat. I mean, he warned me when we first met that he doesn't date because he will always put work first. Why am I shocked when he's done the one thing he promised—put work first?

'I'll make it up to you,' he says as someone talks to him in the background. 'I've got to go. Order something in for yourself. Speak later.'

I hang up and look at myself in the mirror. All dressed up and nowhere to go. Maybe Eloise is free? I ring her but she says she's already out on a date. I don't know why she's answering her phone on a date, but I suppose she's another one constantly stuck to it.

Oh well. I settle down on the sofa, still dressed up to the nines and click onto Netflix. I know I'm in a mood because I don't fancy watching anything and my watch list is huge. I'm too sad, my chest aching. My heart longing for everything and getting nothing.

My phone pings with a text and I grab it hoping its Eloise changing her mind. Instead I see it's Josh.

Hey, how are you? Wondered if you fancied a drink or dinner tonight? x

Damn, how is it he can read my mind? I shouldn't go out with him, I know I shouldn't. Especially dressed up like I am. It's disloyal to Arthur who is just trying to do his job. Trying to make this country a better place. But... well, it feels such a waste to be this dressed up when for once I don't feel the crushing fatigue fighting at my eyelids.

Oh fuck it. It's just dinner with an old friend.

―――――――

WE'VE GONE to Pizza Express at his suggestion. He remembers how much I love those dough balls. I don't just think it's just me, it's the whole nation, but whatever. It's nice to go to just a normal casual restaurant where I can relax and be myself.

'So did you really dress up like this just for me?' he asks with an amused grin.

I sigh, my chest aching again. 'No, I was planning on going out with Arthur,' I admit, twirling my engagement ring round my finger.

'So why aren't you out with him?' he asks, seeming genuinely concerned.

That's one word I'd use to describe Josh: genuine.

I sigh again. 'He had to work. He does a lot of that; work.' I nod manically as if trying to convince myself that it's okay.

He smiles in sympathy. 'But not too much, right. Like, you and the baby are a priority I'm sure.'

My eyes suddenly sting with unshed tears and my chest tightens. I know the truth and it's not the answer he's expecting. It's not even the answer I want to be true.

'Yeah,' I lie, nodding again. 'I'm sure, of course we are. He's just an important man with an important job.'

He smiles kindly. 'I'm sure he'll cut back his hours when the baby is born.'

'I doubt it,' I say absentmindedly while I dip my dough ball in the garlic butter.

'Really?' His eyes widen in shock. 'And you're okay with that?'

I shrug, already resigned to my situation. 'To be honest I don't have much choice. It is what it is.'

He laughs. 'Quoting Love Island. I remember how much you loved that show.'

I giggle. 'And you'd always tease me about it. But I know you loved all those girls in bikinis.'

He smiles affectionally back at me. There's something between us but it's the past, not the future. A feeling of familiarity.

'So, what about you?' I ask, eager to change the subject. 'Are you seeing anyone?'

He shakes his head. 'No. There was a girl a couple of months back, but we just didn't work. Too different.'

Damn, do I know about different people trying to have a relationship.

'That shocks me,' I admit. 'I mean you're such an eligible bachelor. All I hear are friends saying there are no good guys left.'

And he's bloody gorgeous too. Don't get me wrong, he's nowhere near as stunning as Arthur. They're on completely different levels. But he's still very attractive.

He smiles sadly. 'I think that's my problem. I'm too much of a good guy. I'm boring. I just want to find someone to spend my life with. Settle down and have a family. Women say they want that, but in truth they want a bad boy.'

'Everyone does love a bastard,' I nod with a mischievous smile. Myself included. 'Maybe you could pretend to be a bastard at the beginning and then ease them in? Make them feel like they've tamed a bad boy. Women love the idea of that.'

He chews on his lip. 'I suppose I could. Could you coach me?'

I laugh. 'Of course. I've known a lot of heartless bastards in my time.'

I'm currently living with one.

18

Saturday 7th November

Charlotte

I haven't been able to stop thinking about dinner with Josh. How different and lovely my life could have been I'd stayed with him and got pregnant by him; had someone I could rely on, really lean on and trust.

Luckily I still managed to get in before Arthur so he's none the wiser. No matter how many times I tell myself it's no big deal, I can't help but feel guilty like I've betrayed him, which is so stupid. We're not even together.

James said she was going to pop round today to discuss the baby shower. I'm barely out of bed at ten a.m. when there's a knock at the door.

'That'll be the troops,' Arthur says sipping from his coffee cup.

I raise my eyebrows. 'Troops? As in more than one person?'

He grins knowingly as he walks to the door and swings it open. James is there but so is his bloody mother. What is she doing here?

'Morning darling,' she says to Arthur giving him a swift kiss on the lips. Do Mums still kiss their adult sons on the lips? That's weird.

James gives Arthur a squeeze. I'm sure you shouldn't greet friends that way, but then maybe I'm just a jealous and irrational bitch.

I look down and realise I'm still in my pyjamas, with bed hair and unbrushed teeth. Meanwhile James is in a cashmere cream sweater that drops sexily showing off her delicate tanned shoulder. She's so naturally glam.

'Oh, hi! I didn't realise you'd be here so early.'

His mum curls her lip up in distaste, clutching at her Louis Vuitton bag like she's going to catch something from me.

'Honestly, Charlotte.' She lowers her voice to a whisper. 'Arthur won't want to come home to *this*. Go.' She shoos me towards the bedroom. 'Go smarten yourself up.'

I grit my teeth and look to Arthur. He shrugs as if to say, *'sorry'* but doesn't say anything to her. Doesn't jump to defend my honour like I know Josh would. I know it's unfair to compare him to Josh. It's just pretty hard not to.

'I've got to go, I'll leave you ladies to it.'

He's leaving me here with them?

He's out the door before I can protest. Damn, he's not even here on weekends. I run into the bedroom and throw on a pale grey lounge set, run a brush through my hair and quickly brush my teeth.

I look at myself in the mirror, ready to face the sharks. I'll do.

I plaster on a fake smile and go into the main room. They're already sat at the breakfast bar, pieces of paper laid out in front of them.

'Would you like any tea or coffee?' I ask, trying to sound helpful. Really I just feel like a member of staff. His mum does act like the queen.

'I'm fine thank you,' James says with a smile, dismissively.

'And I'm only drinking chamomile right now,' his mum says without looking at me.

I make myself a coffee and join them, feeling like the awkward new girl at school.

'Right,' James says, shuffling her papers. 'We've already discussed a Moon and Stars theme, but we didn't talk about a venue.'

'I'm still not sure about the theme,' Linda muses. 'Does it scream tacky?'

James shakes her head adamantly. 'Not the way we're going to do it. It'll be classy, trust me.'

Linda smiles back at her fondly. 'Oh, I do trust you, James.' She looks briefly at me in distaste.

Do not cry, Charlotte. It's no big deal. She's just a woman. *Not everyone is going to like you and you need to be okay with that.*

'Good, so, the venue,' James says, as if conducting a board meeting. 'I was thinking the Corinthia hotel, but then I wondered if we'd fit everyone in.'

I splutter my coffee. 'How many people are we talking here? I just assumed you'd want to have a few people round here?'

James scoffs a laugh. 'Don't be ridiculous, Charlotte.

This is your baby shower. It needs to be celebrated properly.'

'Especially since Arthur won't let us throw you an engagement party,' Linda adds with a pointed stare.

He won't? Why wouldn't he want an engagement party? But then I suppose he doesn't want to advertise that we're newly engaged while I'm pregnant. Or maybe he doesn't want to celebrate it because it's not true.

'So how many people are we talking?' I ask, my temperature skyrocketing.

'Well, let's see,' Linda muses out loud. 'I want Marge and the girls to be there.'

'Sorry, who is Marge?' I interrupt. I've never even heard of her.

She glares at me. 'They're family friends. Women that have known Arthur *years.*'

She accentuates the word *years,* as if to rub in that I'm just a new novelty. Someone that doesn't know *'her Arthur'* at all, let alone well enough to be having a baby with him.

My muscles tighten with worry. This baby shower is getting carried away.

'I was hoping for a smaller more intimate affair.' I try to straighten myself up.

His mum scoffs. 'There will be no such intimate affair with my son. You've already seen the public interest in him. Imagine if they found out we held it in some back room. We'd be the laughing stock.'

Tad dramatic.

'Okay.' I sigh, quickly relenting. It's easier to try and keep her happy. God knows I need as many points as possible. 'My mum will want to come too.'

James nods. 'I assumed. And your friend Eloise. Do you have any other friends you'd like to invite?'

'Well, seen as we're doing a big thing, yes. I'll make a list.'

I mean, why not show off that I'm having a baby. Especially if it's going to be some Pinterest worthy big affair. I would never imagine something like this normally.

'Great, so we'll book the ballroom at the Corinthia and send invitations immediately.'

They start talking amongst themselves and it's as if I'm not even here. For the first time in my life I understand what it means to be in a room with people but to still feel lonely. I just hope this isn't an insight into my future.

Sunday 8th November

Arthur

I'm already up, showered and dressed by the time Charlotte opens her eyes. She's adorable when she sleeps. All spread out like a cute little starfish. This close I can inspect the freckles on her cheeks without her asking me why I'm staring.

'Are you watching me sleep?' she asks groggily, pushing her hair away from her face. I can't help but smile at her. Busted. 'Because that's creepy.'

'I never claimed it wasn't,' I answer as I sit down next to her. 'How did you sleep?'

'Ugh, like a log. For some reason I always sleep better with you.' Her eyes widen and her cheeks redden when she realises what she's said.

It's amazing to feel so needed. I've always feared relationships because I didn't want anyone to rely on me, but with Charlotte I want that trust. Especially because she seems so hesitant to give it to me.

'I mean... just having a warm body, you know.'

I clutch at my heart. 'And there I was thinking it's because you liked me.'

'Hey,' she points down at her little swollen stomach, 'it's pretty obvious I liked you at some point.'

I snort a laugh. 'But not anymore?'

She starts fidgeting. I hate making her feel uncomfortable, but I really want to hear the answer to this question. The last thing I want is for her to feel like she has to have affection for me just because she's having my baby. But each day that I grow more attached to her the more terrified I am that she'll leave.

'Anyway, I thought today we could maybe pop out to lunch?'

Make up for all of my bad behaviour.

She sighs. 'Yeah, but can we just go somewhere casual this time?'

Yet again I'm reminded how special and unique she is. I'm so lucky she came barrelling into my life.

I nod. 'That's fine by me.'

THAT'S how we find ourselves at an American burger bar in Hampstead. We're sat in a huge green booth facing each other. The smell of grease is in the air, but I know the food is good here. It's my go to for cheat day. She looks gorgeous in a tight burnt orange dress, which shows off the bump, a loose cream cardigan over it. I love when people can clearly see she's pregnant; the cave man in me wants everyone to know my baby is in there.

'So how is work really going?' I ask as we wait for our food.

She shrugs, but I can see from her guarded eyes that there's more to what she's about to say.

'Fine. Stressful, but fine.'

'That's what I'm worried about,' I admit. I hate the thought of her being stressed and I know for a fact that Roger can be a miserable bastard.

'Do you think you're up to it?' I ask carefully.

She scoffs, narrowing her eyes. 'You don't think I can handle the job?' I sense hurt in her voice.

'No, that's not it at all. I'm just worried it's going to stress you out. Stress out the baby.'

Her face drops even further. 'I'm not putting the baby in danger. If I thought that I was, even for one second, I'd do something.'

Oh god, this isn't going well.

'No, of course,' I quickly say, trying to calm her. Everything is coming out wrong. 'I'm just worried is all.'

She raises her chin defiantly. 'Well, there's nothing to worry about. I need to work so there's no point even discussing this.'

'Well...'

'Well what?' She frowns back at me.

I can't help but become a caveman around her. I just want to drag her away to safety where she can grow our baby in peace and tranquillity.

'You could always take early maternity leave.'

Her jaw tenses. Uh-oh. Wrong thing to say.

'Arthur, I've only been there five minutes. It would be highly unprofessional. Not to mention stupid. How would I cope with no money so early? I want to have the full year off with the baby, ideally.'

Where has this come from? Why can't she lean on me? God knows I can't do a lot of things, but the one thing I *can* do is financially support us.

'You keep talking like you're some single mother,' I snap. It's starting to get to me. 'We're in this as a team. I can support you both.'

She turns her nose up at this. 'No offence but I don't want to be supported. I'm not some little trophy wife to be kept at home.'

'No, that's not what I meant,' I quickly interrupt, but apparently she's on a roll.

'I want to be able to earn my own money, not have to ask you for permission every time I want to buy a chocolate bar.'

Who starts an argument over a chocolate bar?

'That's not what I'm saying.'

'So what are you saying?' she challenges, her jaw hard.

'Well...' Shit, she's got me confused. How is it I can be questioned by the Prime Minister and can think on my feet, but she throws me completely for a loop with these mental mood swings. 'I'm just saying that it's an option.'

She crosses her arms over her chest. 'Well, thanks, but no thanks.'

Our burgers arrive, thank God. It's the first time she's smiled in a solid five minutes.

'So, how is the planning for the baby shower going?' I ask, eager to change the subject. I bite into my burger. I'm interested to find out her opinion of James too. God knows she's trying.

She bites into her burger, as if playing for time. While chewing her face drops, eyes widening, her lips twist.

'Oh god,' she barely whispers, putting the burger back on the plate.

'What's wrong?' I ask, leaning over to her. Is the chicken raw?

She opens up her burger. 'They put mayo in it.'

Dammit, we specifically told the waitress no mayonnaise. A tear drops down her cheek, quickly followed by another. Oh my god. They've pushed her over the edge with mayonnaise.

'Don't worry. I'll sort it.'

I summon the waitress over. Damn this restaurant making her upset. It's the last thing I need right now.

'Sorry, but we specifically told you she didn't want mayonnaise and yet it still came with it. What's going on here?'

She grimaces apologetically. 'I'm sorry, sir.' She looks to Charlotte. 'Would you like a replacement?'

'No.' Her voice breaks on a sob. 'It's all ruined now.'

The waitress' eyes widen in panic. 'It would be no problem. I can ask the chef to push it to the front of the queue.'

'I said I don't want it,' she sobs, so loudly we're drawing attention from the other diners.

Way to make a scene. I'm panicking now, my neck hot. I don't do well with weeping females. Never have.

'Which is why you should have ensured it was correct the first time,' I practically growl. Damn woman is trying to ruin my life.

'Don't shout at her,' Charlotte snaps, quickly turning her anger on me. 'Is that how you're going to shout at our child?'

My mouth drops open. Who is this aggressive woman before me? I sure as hell don't recognise her. And insinuating I'm going to be some sort of abusive father. It hurts.

'Charlotte.' My own cheeks are reddening now.

She stands up, throwing her napkin to the table. 'I'm going home.' She turns and storms out.

I stand, take out some cash to leave and then chase after her. I catch up to her in only a few short strides. Lucky for me she only has little legs.

'Charlotte, please.'

'Please, what?' she shouts over the busy traffic, tears falling thick and fast down her cheeks.

I run my hand through my hair. 'Please just calm down so we can talk about this.'

'That's my problem, isn't it, Arthur?' Her chin wobbles. 'I'm just a lowly educated, hysterical woman ruled by my emotions.'

'I never said that!' I shout

She shakes her head. 'You didn't have to. It's obvious.'

'I just think we need to talk this through rationally. You might have grown up in a household of arguing but I definitely didn't.'

Her face drops. I regret it the moment it leaves my lips.

'Arguing?' Her lip trembles. 'How would you know about me growing up around arguing?'

Shit, shit, shit.

'You... you said that they were divorced, I just assumed, I guess.' I can't look her in the eye. I'm such a shit liar.

She studies my face, her eyebrows fused together.

'Tell me the truth, Arthur. I think I at least deserve that.'

I put my hands in my pockets and stare at my feet.

'You looked into me, didn't you?'

I look up to her face. 'Yes, but only because I needed to know if you had any skeletons in your closet.'

Her face falls. 'You couldn't just ask me?'

'Well...'

'You could have, but you didn't know me from Adam."

Her chest hitches. "You didn't know if you could trust me.' She mashes her lips together, nodding in resigned understanding.

God, I hate that I've hurt her.

'Please, Charlotte. Understand that—'

'I do understand,' she interrupts. 'Why don't you go and have a baby with James? She's far more suited to your needs.'

Where the hell did that come from? She starts walking away again.

I catch up to her. 'Charlotte, what does this have to do with James?'

She sniffs. 'Everything and nothing, Arthur. Everything and nothing.' She turns and walks away, only stopping to shout back 'I'm going home. Please give me some time on my own.'

Well fuck. And to think I just wanted a nice lunch.

Charlotte

I feel like a total fucking idiot for so many reasons. I mean, first I cried over mayonnaise. I was damn starving and I still decided to throw a hissy fit and storm out of the restaurant.

I also feel like a fool because what I said had a lot of truth in it. In Arthur's world I'm always going to feel like the lesser person. The thick girlfriend. Even though I'm not even his girlfriend, I'm just his fake fiancé who also happens to be carrying his baby. God, if this baby wasn't in my stomach he wouldn't have given me a second look after our night together.

Having him look into my background has just confirmed all of my worries. He doesn't trust me and probably never will. I'll always be the woman that trapped him with a baby.

I feel such a fool for wishing things could be different. We're polar opposites and it's never going to work. He's suited to someone like James. I should try a bit harder to be civil with her if she's going to inevitably become my child's step mum. God, just the idea of that has my heart hurting.

I need to get it through my thick head that the best I can hope for with him is for a friendship. A civil friendship so that we can both care for our baby in peace. I don't want my baby growing up around arguments like I did. Fearing its parent's moods.

It's he or she who I should be worrying about. Not whether I have bloody mayo in my burger.

The dress I wore today is far too tight to be comfortable, I just want to get changed into my flannel pjs and slob on the sofa watching some sad romantic comedies to give myself a good cry. Only I can't do that. This is his flat and he doesn't want to come home to that. Not only that, but I don't feel like this is enough of my home to be able to do that.

I still feel like a guest in this place. I go into the bedroom and change into my pyjamas, flicking the TV on and deciding to settle down in here. At least I'm out of the way. The TV is on a news channel and they're droning on about worrying terrorism links found in the UK.

Then it dawns on me that this is probably one of the reasons Arthur is so stressed. The man is under so much pressure and then he's having to deal with my mood swings. That's it. Its decided. I have to get it through my head that this arrangement we have is purely of flat mates who happen to be having a baby together.

I promise myself that I won't make this man's life harder than it already is.

19

Arthur

I went into work, not knowing how much time alone she wants. Whether she could stand to look at me. She must think after meeting James that James is my ideal woman and she's just the consolation prize. She couldn't be further from the truth. But we're not even together. Not properly.

She's been willing to lie to her friends and family about us. I am asking a lot of her and the poor woman is pregnant with my kid. She must have all sorts of hormones jumping around that body. I google the size of the baby and read that its already the size of a zucchini. Jesus. I read on to discover that at this stage she's probably suffering from heartburn, trouble sleeping, swelling, general discomfort and shortness of breath. The poor woman. I need to be more careful with what I say to her and how I say it.

By the time I get back to the apartment its early evening. I stick my head round the door expecting to find her on the sofa. She's not there. Panic lances through my veins at the sudden thought that she could have left and gone back to that house share in Watford. The thought of not seeing her until our child is born has my chest squeezing so tight it's a struggle to breathe.

Then I make out the soft snores coming from the bedroom. I've never been so happy to hear those snores.

I tiptoe in there to find her sleeping amidst packets of crisps and Malteser packets, the TV on some shitty romcom. God, she's cute. Even when she's snoring her head off, mouth agape. I hate that she's had to resort to junk food.

I can't work out if she's more beautiful when she's dressed up to kill or make up free in her pyjamas.

I take the remote and turn it off. She startles awake, eyes wide in alarm.

'Shh, it's only me,' I whisper.

She clutches at her chest, as if I almost gave her a heart attack.

'Have you eaten?' I try not to look over the junk food wrappers.

She shakes her head, looking guiltily down at the bed. 'No mayo burgers.'

I bark a laugh, glad she's attempted to break the ice. She smiles shyly up at me.

'I'm sorry for being such a head case. These hormones are turning me into a crazy woman. I swear I'm normally not like this.'

I sit down on the edge of the bed. 'I get it. I'm asking an awful lot of you right now.'

She shrugs, but I can see now, looking so closely into those hazel eyes that the responsibility weighs heavily on her shoulders.

'But we're a team, right?'

She nods. 'We are. But...' She worries her lip.

'But what?'

She fidgets with her necklace. 'I just think we should keep things a bit clearer. Put this back to as much of a business arrangement as we can.'

I frown, but quickly try to recover. *Business arrangement?* She's kind of right, of course. There's too many blurred lines between us. It's all too tempting for me to reach over in bed at night and touch her skin. Pull her under my arm. Spoon her. Wrap my arms around her swelling belly.

'I'll sleep on the sofa from now on,' I offer.

She sits up. 'No, I can't ask you to do that.'

'You're not asking, I'm insisting.'

I plan on making this as easy as possible for her.

'I can't expect you to sleep on that sofa and then get up for a full day's work. Why don't I just get a bed for the spare room?'

'That's the baby's room.' I don't like this. Something deep in my gut tells me this isn't right. She's slipping through my fingers right in front of me.

'Well, it makes sense for me to be in there with it anyway. That way you can get a full night's sleep.'

I don't think I'll be able to sleep without her anyway. How is it I've found such a selfless woman in a sea of manipulative gold diggers?

'Look, we'll sort it out later. For now, I'll take the sofa.'

I couldn't care less where I sleep. For once someone else's happiness is paramount to mine.

Friday 13th November

Charlotte – 30 Weeks Pregnant

I got myself a single bed delivered for the spare room. Arthur says he's fine sleeping on the sofa, but I do notice him cracking his neck. That sofa is killing him, but he's too proud or stubborn to admit it.

I've decided to take myself shopping where I can also pick up a duvet and some new bed sheets. Make my bedroom a bit cosier. I'm also craving some fatty food. It's funny the things you miss when you have everything taken care of for you. I miss scanning the aisles and treating myself to a chocolate dessert. Checking out the specials and sales. Especially with all the healthy food he has in the apartment.

So today I'm having a wander round and enjoying my time. I pass the dog food aisle and I don't know why, but I get the sudden craving to want to eat it. What the hell is wrong with me?

I must just be craving stew. I go down to the meat aisle but everything I look at makes my stomach churn. I don't know why, I'm hardly a vegetarian but ugh. I just can't do it.

I browse round the rest of the shop, all the while feeling drawn to the dog food. Dammit, why do I want it? Maybe I need to be checked into a mental health facility. Get some sort of evaluation.

There's no harm in me just walking down the aisle. Maybe I'll be able to smell it from there.

Now I'm at the cans.

Jesus the urge to just open one up and sniff it is strong.

Indescribably strong. Is this a pregnant thing? Or have I had a breakdown?

I have a quick look around me and the coast seems clear. I just need to sniff it. I'm sure I'll be so disgusted I'll never go near it again. I break one free from the plastic packaging and peel off the top of a can. I sniff it, but instead of finding it disgusting it smells delicious to me. God, how I want to eat it, but I just can't. Thank God I'm not *that* barmy.

Oh well. At least I had a sniff.

'Charlotte?'

My stomach bottoms out. Too fucking late.

I throw the tin back onto the shelf but in my haste it rolls off and smacks against the floor. I look up to follow where the food has exploded and there stands Arthur's mother and two friends. Sprayed in dog food.

'What on earth, Charlotte?' She says, grabbing tissues out of her bag and passing some to her friends.

They look on in horror, meaty chunks in their hair.

What a way to be introduced to your friend's fake daughter in law.

'I'm so sorry.'

My cheeks are on fire. Why? Why was I doing that?

'What on earth were you doing with open dog food?' Linda demands. 'It looked like you were about to eat it.'

I force a laugh, but it comes out more of a squeal.

'Of course not! I was just... I was inspecting it.'

'Inspecting it?' She repeats in disbelief, dabbing at her Chanel jacket. 'Why on earth would you be inspecting it?'

Think Charlotte, think. Now is not the time for baby brain to kick in.

'Because... because I've heard some mixed reviews about their quality and... and I wanted to see for myself.'

She narrows her eyes at me. 'But you don't even have a dog?'

She's right. Why would I be concerned when I don't have a dog? I have to think here. I don't doubt she'd jump at the first opportunity to have me locked up in a psych ward.

'Well... we're considering getting one.'

Her face scrunches up in revulsion. 'Sorry, you think that just before having a baby you should get a puppy? Are you mad?'

I grimace. 'Well, obviously I'm doing my research into it first. Hence the dog food.'

She nods, unconvinced. 'Well at least you're being thorough, but may I suggest you talk this through with Arthur. It's a very big commitment.'

Whereas getting married and having a baby isn't. Yeah right.

'Will do.' I salute her, turn and run the fuck away as quickly as I can.

Saturday 14th November

Charlotte

I've somehow talked Arthur into going shopping again. Not to the supermarket, thank goodness, but baby shopping. I don't think I can go back to that particular supermarket ever again. I mean what if they have security cameras down that aisle? I bet I gave them a great laugh. Arthur was so confused, asking why his mum thought we were getting a puppy. I had to bullshit and say she misheard me.

I've promised him I won't cause an incident of any kind. Yeah, like I can really make those kinds of promises. I haven't got a crystal ball and I apparently have zero control over this pregnant body.

It's already bloody stressful and we haven't even left the car yet. There seems to be absolutely no parking spaces.

'It's everyone doing their bloody Christmas shopping,' Arthur whinges as we go round again in the hope that someone's left. 'All I seem to hear is how everything is online nowadays. How the high street is struggling. Well every fucker is here today.'

I snort a laugh. He's so cute when he's moody. His ears go red and his jaw hard. He glares at me, but I can see the pulling at the edges of his lips. He wants to smile and I love that I can bring that silliness out of him.

A smart car pulls out of a space in front of us.

'There!' I shout triumphantly. Finally.

He speeds over but then pauses to assess it, chewing on his lip.

'I'll reverse in.'

Now that I look closer it is a tight spot. I'm not sure if we'll fit in.

He grimaces, chewing on his bottom lip. 'No offence, but I'm not sure you'll get out once I've parked, so maybe get out here and guide me in?'

'So what you're saying is I'm a whale?' I glare at him, really more amused than angry. It's true, I've really popped recently. Everything is starting to feel squashed. I'm not sure someone of my frame was ever meant to carry a big bastard baby of his.

He sighs, scrubbing his hand over his face. 'I never said that.'

'It's fine.'

I really need to stop winding him up. He's stressed

enough as it is. I must tell him to get his blood pressure checked.

Like a trooper, I get out and then start guiding him back with his windows down. Another two cars are waiting for us now. Way to add to the pressure. I'm starting to sweat. Everything makes me sweat nowadays. That whole pregnancy glow bullshit is really just us being slick and shiny with perspiration.

'Straighten up, now left, now—'

I hear a crunch and at first don't understand what's happened. Until I look down and see that he's driven over my fucking foot! The wheel bumps off it. I jump back and scream hopping on my good leg. An ear-splitting scream that I don't even recognise as my own erupts from my lips. I fall back against the other car, wailing for him to stop.

He jumps out of the car, his eyes bulging out of their sockets when he takes in the scene.

'Charlotte? What the hell happened?'

'Foot. Ran. Foot,' is all I can make out to him. The pain is blinding, taking over every cell of my body. I can't even think straight.

The other cars start to beep impatiently. Can't they see this is a medical emergency? Arseholes.

He bends down to unzip my caramel suede boot. I scream out from the slightest touch, slapping him away from me like a crazed woman.

'Shit.' His face drains of all colour, his eyes blinking rapidly. 'We need to get you to a hospital.'

'Yeah, no shit, Sherlock!'

20

Wednesday 18th November

Charlotte – 31 Weeks Pregnant

I've fractured my foot. Or should I say *Arthur* has fractured my foot. Stupid bastard. I have crutches for six bloody weeks and let me tell you, being pregnant and on crutches is hard.

It's an added chore when you have to explain to everyone what happened. More humiliating when the gossip magazines start tweeting about it and its discussed on Good Morning Britain.

Sometimes I wish he'd run me completely over and killed me. I joke. I'm just being dramatic.

Arthur has been amazing, in his guilt he's treated me like a queen, which I bloody need. I've gone from an independent woman to a disabled person that needs help doing everything. It would be humiliating in front of anyone, let alone a guy they barely know.

He tried to talk me out of work, claiming again I should take early maternity leave. I told him no, that I wanted to work.

It's a lie; I don't want to work. Does anyone? Well, maybe I'd want to work if it was doing what I loved. Not dealing with the psychopath that is Roger. But regardless, I don't want to start my maternity leave so early.

A huge part of me is still waiting for the bottom to fall out of this arrangement. For Arthur to realise he doesn't want a live-in family he never asked for. If he comes to that conclusion before the baby is born I want to be independent enough to afford to raise this baby. I want as long as possible with it before I have to go back to work which is looking the more likely option.

Mum's even talking about going down to two days so she can come up to help look after it. It's stuff I don't want to think about but know that I might have to. I'm not sure if she really meant it though. She was apologising because she can't make the baby shower. I don't know what's more important than your first grandchild, but there you go.

Maybe the saddest thing of all is that thanks to the crutches I've had to kiss goodbye to my heels far earlier than I'd planned. I only own one pair of flat black ballet pumps so I intend to do some serious internet shopping tonight, even if I can only wear one. I feel so frumpy in flats. It does nothing for my legs and I've had to cover my toes from the cast with a black sock. Not exactly professional to have your toes hanging out at work.

Roger has had next to no sympathy. Said I'll have to ask someone else to make his coffees as obviously I can't hop back with it from the kitchen.

I'm just writing up a report for him when I feel a pain around my stomach. A sort of tightening, like someone is pulling a band around it. That's weird. I thought I had enough to worry about with my palms aching and the muscles under my armpits killing me.

I carry on but after a while I get another. It's not painful enough to be worrying. I've felt more for a period pain. Maybe I just need a trip to the toilet.

I hurry in there as quickly as I can and have a quick wee. When I wipe myself I freeze, staring down at the tissue paper stained with a spot of bright red blood in it. Shit.

I stare back at it for what must be minutes. That *is* blood, right? I'm not imagining it. I place it on the floor in front of me, sure my eyes must be playing tricks on me. I grab a fresh piece of tissue and dab myself. Another spot. I lay it on the floor.

Before long I have seven pieces of loo roll on the floor, each with their own small spot of blood. Okay now I'm panicking. What the fuck could be wrong? I'm only thirty-one weeks. The scan at the hospital after the accident showed the baby was okay.

I need to stay calm, but my pulse is hammering, my throat pinching from not bursting into tears. Stay calm and get the book they tell us to take everywhere. Call the number and ask them what to do. Hopefully I won't get the same nurse from blow job gate.

I rush back to my desk, nearly catching my crutches on a piece of flooring and landing on my face. I call and tell them as quietly as possible what's happening. They tell me to come straight into triage. This still doesn't feel real. Like I'm in a distant nightmare.

Now just to tell Roger.

I struggle to his door, balance myself on the door frame

to knock and walk in before waiting for an answer.

'Yes?' he asks, his tone sharp.

'Hi.' I grimace a smile. 'I'm going to have to go to hospital. I'm... I'm bleeding.'

Just saying it out loud again has me feeling hysterical. No, Charlotte, this is fine. Everything is going to be fine.

'Okay,' he nods, not the smallest bit concerned. 'But before you go could you please call Jacob in IT and tell him we'll have to reschedule our meeting to tomorrow.'

I nod, turning around to leave. Hang on a minute. What am I doing? I just told the guy I'm bleeding. My baby could be dying right now and he's more worried about a bloody meeting. It's time I stand up for myself.

'Actually... I'll do it after I get back from the hospital. I *am* bleeding so I think that takes precedence.'

He nods, the chords in his neck tensed. The guy is a grade one arsehole.

I try calling Arthur as I walk out, but holding a phone and crutches together is near on impossible. When I finally get a cab I try again. It's going straight to voicemail. I call his PA and ask him to call me when he's out of his meeting.

I'm sure it's nothing anyway.

I'M in triage and they've attached my bump to a machine which is measuring something that is printing out on a chart. I keep hearing women all around me being told that they're suffering from Braxton hicks, a totally normal part of pregnancy, and that they can go home and not worry.

I know they're going to say the same to me. I'll be just as embarrassed as the rest of them. But at least I can get home. I hate hospitals and being pregnant, I can smell every single thing in here. Even the tuna pasta salad the woman in the cubicle next to mine had for lunch.

A cheery nurse comes to check on my chart. I smile, hoping she'll be nice to me when I get embarrassed for wasting their time. God knows how busy the NHS is and I'm laid up here being stupid.

'I'm actually feeling better.'

She nods, still looking at the form, her expression levelling out to an eventual grimace. 'Well, it seems that you're having three contractions every ten minutes.'

I wait for her to finish, to tell me its Braxton hicks. But she doesn't.

'But that's normal right. Braxton hicks?'

She purses her lips, not looking at me. 'No, these aren't Braxton hicks. These are real contractions showing on the chart. I'm going to talk to the doctor.'

She smiles and leaves, pulling the curtain around me. Shit, why is she pulling the curtain? I thought you only had contractions when you were giving birth? I can't be giving birth. I'm only thirty-one weeks. It's miles too early.

The curtain pulls and an Indian doctor in his fifties appears with the nurse. That was bloody quick. Why so quick? Are they worried? Should I be more concerned?

'Hello, Miss Bellswain.' He takes the chart and looks over it. Then he places his hands on my stomach and feels around.

'Right, I'd like to do a scan.'

Another nurse brings in some weird looking portable machine.

'Scan? Do you think the baby is in trouble?' I don't recognise my own wobbly voice.

Dear God, if I lose this baby I won't be able to cope. It's the only thing I'm sure about.

He smiles briefly. 'No, but we'd like to check to see if the baby is breach.'

I snort a laugh. 'But I'm thirty-one weeks. I'm not having my baby for ages. That gives it months to turn, right?'

So why are they worried now?

He squirts some cold jelly onto my stomach and starts prodding with the wand, pressing a lot harder than my previous scans. It's heartbeat echoes around the room. Phew. Thank God it's okay.

'We're worried you're in premature labour. If we are forced to deliver we'll need to know. Ah.' He points at the screen. 'Breach as I thought.'

'Which means?' I'm losing it now. You can hear it in my voice. The hysteria is here to stay. Goosepimples have risen down my arms, the hair on the back of my neck standing up.

He purses his lips. 'If we're forced to deliver you'd have to have a c-section.'

'C-section?!' I shriek. What the fuck is going on here? 'The baby is too small. It's too early.'

Fuck. *Fuck.*

He smiles briefly. 'Please don't panic, Miss Bellswain. For now, I want to admit you onto the ward so we can monitor you overnight. See if your contractions peter out by themselves or if they increase.'

Okay, so there is a chance they'll stop by themselves.

'What if they increase?'

'We can give you some medication to slow down the labour and some steroids to build up the babies lungs. They're not developed yet and ideally we'd like to get you to week thirty-four at the earliest.'

This guy is wrong. Now is clearly the time to panic. I can't give birth to a premature baby that's lungs haven't developed yet. Will it survive without proper lungs? And even if it does are we looking at a lifetime of problems ahead of us?

'I know this is a lot right now, but please don't worry. We'll put you on codeine for the pain. All you have to concentrate on is relaxing yourself.'

Easy for him to say.

'Was this brought on by the accident?' I ask, pointing down to my fractured foot.

He nods. 'Potentially. But it's important not to blame yourself. This could have happened for a number of reasons.'

But it *could* be my fault. Well mine and Arthur's fault.

I try to call Arthur again as they wheel my bed into a lift and transport me to a ward, but again it goes to voicemail. They drop me off in a room with three other pregnant women of varying stages and ask me to do a urine sample.

I try to call his PA again, but a nurse tells me that phones aren't allowed on the ward and that I have to turn it off. I quickly type a text message and shoot it off to Arthur and Eloise before begrudgingly turning it off. I hope to God the message gets through.

Arthur

Its past nine p.m. by the time I get out of the meeting. There was a scandal with a minister who was forced to resign so we had to do a reshuffle. It sounds far easier than it is. Naturally someone is promoted, but that causes a domino effect of having to fill all of the other positions.

Exhausted I retrieve my phone from the cubby hole as I leave number ten. I need to call Charlotte. She must be getting sick of my coming home so late. I know I am.

I've never felt so bad in my entire life. I still can't believe

I ran over her foot. For fucks sakes. Six weeks on crutches is going to kill her. She'll have them right up to thirty-seven weeks. She'll be huge by then and having to struggle around on crutches. I can't believe I'm such an idiot.

I don't think I'll ever forgive myself. But the thing that scared me the most is that I hurt the woman I'm... God, I don't even know how I feel. I'm a mess.

I turn my phone on to call her and see she's rang me three times. Eloise has rung me seventeen times. What the hell is going on? I ring Charlotte back immediately, my heart racing. It goes straight to voicemail. Damn. I see she's also sent me a message.

Been admitted to a ward in maternity. Don't panic but they say I'm having contractions and might be going into premature labour. x

Oh and the baby is breach. x

What the actual fuck Charlotte?

I grab my coat and run out into the street, hailing a cab. I ring Eloise after shouting to the driver to take me to the hospital as fast as he can.

'About fucking time,' she snaps as soon as it connects.

I'm not used to staff speaking to me like this.

'Eloise, what happened?'

'Ugh, I know about as much as you. I called the hospital and they won't tell me anything because I'm not family. What a joke.

'Don't worry I'm heading there now.'

'Good. Report back, Arthur. She shouldn't be going through this alone.'

And yet she'll go through so much alone when she's with me. I'll always let her down.

It hurts my heart to admit.

'I will.'

I eventually get to the hospital where I'm directed to the maternity ward but warned that visiting times are over. Yeah, like they're going to stop me.

I finally get to the maternity ward after following ridiculous coloured arrows on the floor and buzz their doorbell.

'Hello?' a tired voice answers.

'Oh, hi. My fiancée got taken in earlier today. I think she's on this ward.'

'What's her name?'

'Charlotte Bellswain.'

There's a pause. 'Yes, she's here but I'm afraid visiting times ended two hours ago.'

'Please. I can't get hold of her.' I'm not above begging.

'Can't bend the rules for anyone, I'm afraid. We've got a lot of pregnant women in here who don't need the added stress.'

What a fucking jobsworth. I'll be writing a letter to her superior.

'Can you at least tell me how she is?'

'She's being monitored overnight. No immediate action is to be taken unless her contractions increase. I can pass on a message if you'd like.'

'Yes, please tell her...'

That I'm scared. That I need to see her face. Need to know the baby is okay. Need to tell her that I'm falling in love with her. Woah, where did that last one come from? I'm not capable of love. I don't have the time or energy to give it.

'Please just tell her I tried to come see her,' I say lamely instead.

'Will do.'

I walk away knowing everything that I want is on the other side of that door.

21

Thursday 19th November

Charlotte

*T*rying to sleep in a hospital is hard with your leg raised by a pillow, the nurses constantly coming in and out to do our observations and being hooked up to this baby monitor that beeps loudly. I've barely drunk any water because detaching myself from it and hobbling down the corridor to the bathroom is such a pain in the arse. It's extremely hard when you know that the man you're falling for doesn't give a shit about you.

I waited all night for him to turn up and reassure me. I waited for no avail. The pain hasn't exactly got worse, but my body is growing tired of it. The tightening's are just being more poorly received.

I have to say though that if this is labour pain, its far better than I feared. The machine measures my tightening's with numbers. Every now and again it goes over a hundred, beeping louder, causing me to panic, but no one comes rushing in.

I want nothing more than to sob hysterically but I can't. Not with the other women on the ward. There's always the risk that someone would recognise me and sell the story. That's the last thing I need.

The doctor finally comes around and checks my chart.

'Right, let's see. And you've had no bleeding since yesterday?'

I shake my head.

'Well the contractions are still coming, but they're not increasing in speed which is a good thing. We'll do a speculum and as long as you're not dilating I'm happy to send you home. As long as you promise to come back if you have any more bleeding or if the tightening's increase in speed.'

I nod. I should be looking forward to leaving, but right now I don't even feel like I have a home. I'm just a house guest for Arthur. An inconvenient grower of his baby that he has to accommodate.

The doctor gives me a speculum, which basically means me opening my legs and him coming at me with a gigantic torch and prod. I really wish I had someone's hand to hold when that happens, but I reassure myself that I'm a strong, independent woman who is capable of doing this alone.

'You're good to go,' he announces. 'I'll send a nurse to discharge you.'

Arthur

I stand outside the maternity ward with a bunch of flowers and a get well soon balloon, counting down the minutes until visiting time. Three more minutes until I can beg for Charlotte's forgiveness. I didn't sleep a wink all night worrying about her.

The door opens and I look up, wondering if they're opening early. Instead I see Charlotte being helped out by a nurse, shuffling on her crutches. She looks pale, dark rings round her eyes from lack of sleep. She's still wearing the same creased clothes as yesterday. Her hazel eyes widen when she spots me. There's vulnerability in them and its then it hits me fully, I've hurt her far more than I ever feared. The strong act she puts on is just that, a façade to protect herself.

'Charlotte.' My voice is pained but it still doesn't communicate how sorry I am. Nothing can.

She walks slowly towards me, pausing to tuck some hair behind her ear.

'I am so sorry, Charlotte. I came here last night but they wouldn't let me in.'

'Really?' Her voice is quiet, her soul downtrodden. I hate seeing her like this.

'They didn't tell you? The nurse said she'd pass it on.'

What a bitch. She clearly has no idea she's playing with people's lives here. Or who I am. I'm going to lodge a formal complaint.

She shrugs.

'These are for you,' I offer lamely, presenting the flowers and balloon. Now I feel stupid for bringing them when she can't even hold them.

'Thanks.' She walks ahead of me, surprisingly fast despite the crutches. 'You can get back to work. They've told me to take another day off.'

I rush after her. She stops at the lifts.

'Charlotte, please forgive me,' I beg, imploring her to look at me.

She shrugs, her eyes not meeting mine. 'There's nothing to forgive, Arthur. You haven't made me any promises.'

My heart sinks. How can she think so little of herself? Of us?

I stand in front of her to halt any quick escape. 'You might not think so, but I have. Damn it, I'll make them right here right now. I promise to always be here for you and the baby.'

She scoffs. 'I wish I could believe you.'

The lift doors open and we both walk in.

'Charlotte, yesterday the message didn't get to me until I was out of the meeting. I rushed straight here but they wouldn't let me in. Please understand, I would have been here in an instant had I known. You should have told my assistant it was an emergency.'

Her head shoots to look at me, her eyes hard. 'Oh, so this is *my* fault. Okay.'

'No, of course not.' I sigh, pulling against my hair. I'm saying everything wrong-again.

'Because silly me, I didn't want to tell your PA that I was bleeding, potentially losing our baby.'

Shit, she was bleeding?

'Why didn't you call and say something when they'd admitted you?'

'Because they told me phones weren't allowed. Most women came in with a partner. Someone to rely on. Meanwhile, I'm on my own while I'm told I might be delivering early. Jesus, they had to give me some spare pyjamas because no one had brought me in a bag. I haven't even brushed my teeth this morning.'

I literally couldn't feel worse. Except then her chin

LAURA BARNARD

wobbles and I know she's going to cry. I step forward just as
she breaks down in tears. I scoop her up and into my arms,
letting her crutches fall to the floor. She sobs onto my chest
while I stroke her hair back off her face.

'I'm so sorry, Charlotte. You and the baby mean so much
to me. More than you'll ever know.'

She pulls back to look up at me, forcing a smile, but I
know, deep down in my chest, that she doesn't believe me.
That it's going to take a hell of a lot of convincing. Now, I'm
more committed than ever in proving that to her.

Monday 23rd November

Charlotte – 32 Weeks Pregnant

Arthur asked me to consider taking early maternity leave
again but I've refused. Yes, I might be on crutches and I
might have had a scare resulting in a hospital visit, but I'm
still perfectly capable.

Well, okay maybe I shouldn't use the word capable. I
need help doing *every* damn thing. It's like having your arms
cut off. I have to shower with a chair and this weird condom
thing over my foot. I now have a weird kind of disabled
trolly I can use to put stuff in and help me from room to
room. James dropped it off, *just trying to help*. Annoyingly it
is helpful, but I feel so unattractive hopping and jumping
around the place. I'm sure that was her intent.

If I'm honest I don't feel up to work. I feel like bursting
into tears whenever Roger even so much as looks at me. Not
just from his resentment at having a pregnant employee, but
from this whole sorry situation I've gotten myself into.

After finally getting to grips with the fact I can't truly

rely on Arthur, I've become more realistic about my situation.

I don't want to trust him or what he can offer us. I want to provide it myself. I've been looking after myself my whole life. I should be good at it.

I'm writing up meeting notes when I get the urge to fart. I could really do with just letting this one slip out. I've got too much work to do to be going to the toilet every time I fart and wee. Especially with the added trauma of hobbling there on crutches with everyone passing me asking if I need some help.

I cannot believe how much wind I'm carrying around these days.

I check around and then slowly relax myself. Only... woah, what's happening here? This isn't a fart at all. This is a shit. I'm going to shit myself. Again.

I suck it back in as best I can, grabbing my crutches and trying my best to hurry up. Only I fall on my foot. Oh crap. Pain radiates up my leg causing me to shriek out loud.

And... I'm pretty sure I just started to shit myself. I struggle with the crutches, pushing past the pain and struggling up and towards the bathroom.

My bowels make an unspeakable noise. I'm sweating now. I can feel my neck is slick with sweat. This can't be happening again.

I finally reach the bathroom, bash the door open, drop the crutches and hike my dress up. Then I let the evil unfold. Whatever happens now it's too late. I've shit myself in a public place. Again. There is no going back from this.

Tuesday 24th November

Charlotte

'I can't go back there. I just can't,' I moan to Eloise on the phone early next morning.

She laughs. 'I don't blame you. Although I don't think many people noticed.'

I sigh. 'El, don't pretend like no one has noticed the crazy disgusting pregnant person I've become.'

She chuckles. 'Okay, people have obviously noticed you've changed. But what I'm saying is that not many people witnessed you shit yourself.'

'Thank God.'

'They did, however, see you leaving in a new dress sobbing hysterically on me. I think that might have done more damage than good.'

'See! It's all so humiliating.'

I just want to crawl into a pit and hide until this baby arrives. God knows I'm not fit for the public.

'So tell Arthur you want to take early maternity leave. He's bloody suggested it about ten times.'

'Yeah, I know. But I made such a huge fuss about not needing to. I hate going back on my word.'

And having to rely on his promises and not myself. This puts a spanner in the works for my independence plans.

'Honestly, don't worry about it. I've got to go. Speak later.'

I get myself into the kitchen, knowing I should be getting ready about now. I hate the thought of letting Roger down, but... God I don't know if I can work there anymore.

It's not just the shitting myself incident, its all of it. The constant anxiety of getting something wrong and pissing Roger off. I realise now that it weighs heavily on me. Maybe that's the reason I went into early contractions. Maybe this is all my own fault.

Arthur walks into the kitchen putting his phone back into his pocket.

'Charlotte, I'd like you to reconsider early maternity leave. I think it should start today.'

I look back at him with raised eyebrows.

'You spoke to Eloise?'

He desperately tries to hide his grin, but I forgive him because he's so cute when he smiles.

'I told her to text me whenever I need to know something.'

I roll my eyes. 'Good to know.'

'Whatever. Stay at home. Rest.'

I know what he's really asking me is to trust him. I desperately want to, but I just don't think I can.

22

Saturday 28th November

Arthur

I've somehow been talked into coming to Ikea with Charlotte. I've tried to get out of it. What women in her right mind wants to go to Ikea with a fractured foot? She found out that you can hire a wheelchair while you're there. She's the one saying she doesn't want to be treated as if she's disabled and now she's wanting to hire a wheelchair. I'll never understand women.

I tried to explain we can order everything online and that we can afford higher end stuff, but apparently she just loves Ikea. Says I have to eat some meatballs while we're there too. Sounds bizarre if you ask me.

We get her into a wheelchair, but she insists she push herself along because we'll need me to push the trolley. Then we're thrust into a strange world of fake rooms.

Charlotte's eyes widen as she wheels from scene to scene, explaining what she likes about each thing. How it would or wouldn't go in the flat. All while being practically sandwiched between other members of the public. The entire population of London must be in here today.

But this behaviour is all tame until we get to the children's section. Her eyes are awe stricken as if she's smoked a blunt. She starts cooing over everything. I have to admit that for a cheap Swedish furniture company they do have some good ideas in here.

She grabs a few things, throwing them in my trolley, and then says we need to go downstairs.

'There's a downstairs?' I ask, unable to hide the horror from my voice.

She nods. 'The basement. It's the best part.'

I gulp but follow her to the lifts. The doors open and I'm overwhelmed by textiles of every colour and texture. She starts throwing stuff in the trolley. Blankets, candles, plants, curtains, rugs. I have no idea where she plans on putting this stuff but she insists *she 'needs it all'*.

I don't know how she's finding the energy for all this. It looks like pushing herself in the wheelchair is actually harder than the crutches. It better not bring on those contractions again.

We have to walk through a hideous warehouse in order to get in the queue for the tills.

'I'm never coming to Ikea again,' I announce on a sigh, stooped over the overflowing trolley.

Her eyes widen. Well, shit. I didn't think she'd be that shocked. She must *really* love Ikea.

'I'm sorry, okay? It's just not a place meant for men.'

'No you idiot,' she whisper hisses. 'I think my waters just broke.'

I look down and the smallest puddle has appeared under her seat.

'Shit! They can't have. You're only thirty-two weeks.'

I knew pushing herself in that wheelchair would exhaust her. Maybe she's been in some sort of slow labour this whole time.

'Oh god, I just knew I'd end up being early. Look, we'll just pay for this and then call the hospital when we get home.'

'I don't bloody think so,' I snap, already looking for our closest exit. 'We're leaving this and going straight to the hospital.'

'But... but... my candles.'

I take her wheelchair and drag her out of the shop.

Tuesday 1st December

Charlotte – 33 Weeks Pregnant

I've felt low since the Ikea incident. We rushed off to hospital to only be told that I'd actually pissed myself. How humiliating. It's a good thing really. Means that there's nothing wrong with the baby. Just that my bladder control has now diminished to nothing.

But learning that kind of information is never something to be jolly about. They made me do a quick urine sample while I was there, and it turns out I was a bit dehydrated. They allowed me home explaining that I have to drink gallons of water a day. Arthur bought me a water bottle with times along the side of it and is constantly bugging me about it now.

On top of the humiliation of peeing myself in Ikea, I also

have the fact that I wasn't able to buy any of the bits I wanted. Those things were going to help me make his apartment feel like mine. I asked Arthur if we could go back but he said no. Didn't have time apparently.

And did I mention I'm still on crutches? I know I did, but I'm so pissed off about it.

Oh well. I'm forcing myself to trudge on. To count my blessings and remember that I could be in far worse situations. Sure, I'm still having to live a lie about being engaged but he's here, although in some of my darkest moments I actually think I'd be better off on my own. Not having to lie, doing everything my own way without having to consult anyone.

I've decided to cheer myself up I'm going to buy myself a mozzarella panini in the local cafe. Just what I need, carbs and cheese.

I've just placed my order and am waiting at a small table when Josh walks in. He spots me immediately and waves, walking over. Is the guy following me or something? I shake my head at the ridiculous idea. I don't own bloody London.

'Hey, how are you?' he asks, his eyes kind.

I sigh involuntarily. 'Yeah, I'm fine. You?'

He frowns. 'Uh-oh. That doesn't sound good. Want to talk about it?'

My soul feels heavy and tired. Or maybe it's my body that feels heavy and tired. I've got a blister on my palm from this torture device crutch.

'No, I'm okay. Just a bit low is all.'

He sits down with a friendly smile. 'Come on. Out with it.'

Damn it, he's always been able to read me so well.

'I'm just... I'm realising how different me and Arthur are.'

I feel like such a traitor for even speaking that out loud. Especially to my ex-boyfriend.

He raises his eyebrows. 'Bit of an understatement.'

'Yeah, I know. It's my own fault.'

'I didn't say that.' He shakes his head.

'We went to Ikea at the weekend and... its stupid, but he just absolutely hated it. I had this idea of us getting excited about buying bits for the flat, for the baby, but he just didn't want to be there.'

'And it makes you think he's not interested?' he asks, seeming genuinely concerned.

'Yeah.' I sigh. 'I guess that's the root of everything.'

Regardless of how he's said he feels about me, there's still that niggle of doubt in the back of my head that tells me he's only here for the baby.

'Plus you don't like relying on people to begin with, so for you to trust him with that and feel let down. I get it.'

'I don't like relying on people?' I repeat back with a frown. 'What makes you say that?'

'It's obvious, Charlotte. Our whole relationship you remained fiercely independent. You didn't want to rely on me for anything.'

I suppose I am like that a little bit. But why rely on people when they'll only let you down? My arguing parents taught me early on that I should be self-reliant. They were always too busy arguing with each other to worry about me. I set my own alarms, I got myself to school.

'Well maybe I'm ready for someone to rely on. It just so happens I've found a man who a lot of other people rely on too.'

He smiles sadly. I feel a surge of guilt for talking about Arthur. He's a good man. Fear grips me at the thought of this getting back to him.

'I shouldn't have said all of this. Please don't repeat it to anyone.'

He squeezes my hand just as my panini is put down in front of me.

'Hey, I'm always here to listen and I'll never repeat anything you say. Just know that some of us can be relied on. Even only as a mate.'

He smiles, stands up, collects his coffee and is about to leave when he leans into me.

'And if you ever need a buddy to go to Ikea with, you know I've always loved that place.'

He goes on his way. Why is it I'm forgetting why I broke up with that man?

Thursday 3rd December

Charlotte

I'm not even two weeks into my maternity leave but I'm bored. I need a project and I've decided doing up baby's nursery will be the perfect distraction. Nesting and all that. I've been sleeping in here so its quickly become an unorganised dumping ground of my stuff. It's been giving me anxiety.

My phone rings and I'm sure it's just Arthur calling me *again* to ask how I am. He's gone completely nuts since the hospital incident. He's forever calling to check I'm okay. I know its sweet and I'm glad he's interested enough to care but, well, I can't help but think he's just worried about the baby. I'm just the human attached to it.

Instead, I find an unknown number calling.

'Hello?' I ask tentatively.

'Hi, is that Charlotte Bellswain?' a posh woman asks.

'Yes.'

'Hi. You probably don't remember me, but I met you at the Civil Service Awards a good few months ago and you gave me your number in case I ever needed a dress designed.'

Oh my god. Of course I remember Alice Elizabeth Du Pont.

'Yes, I remember'

'Well, I have an event a week Saturday. It's black tie. I did have another dress planned but I've just tried it on and I'm not happy with it. It would be a quick turnaround, but do you think you could do it?'

'Of course! I would absolutely love to!'

Saturday 5th December

I can't believe I have the chance to design a dress for Alice Elizabeth Du Pont. Whatever she wears is talked about in the press. It's a huge opportunity for me. I already have some ideas I've jotted down in my journal. I can't wait to meet her and get started, even if it will be a nightmare while I'm on crutches.

Arthur of course went mad and said I shouldn't be stressing my body out designing a dress, but I told him this opportunity was too big to turn down. He eventually agreed.

In the meantime I have my baby shower. It's been turned into such a dramatic circus it's nothing like I wanted myself, but it was easier to let James plough on ahead.

As I hobble into the hotel and take in the grand surroundings my stomach churns with nervous anticipation. Arthur reaches down to my crutch and squeezes my hand reassuringly. I look down at it, so grateful he's here. His phone rings, so he drops my hand to answer.

'There you are!'

I look up to see James waving at me from across the room. She's wearing a silver dress with intricate gold stars sewn on it. Her brunette glossy hair cascades beautifully down her lean back. She's so damn gorgeous. It makes me sick. I feel like such a frump in my navy wrap dress and flat matching ballet pump and sock next to her. Arthur says I'm mad, but I know I've started to get puffy in my face.

I force a smile, take a deep breath and make my way over to her. She embraces me in her arms like she's known me for years, air kissing me. She takes me into the ballroom, past the gold and white balloon arch, complete with stars, and giant sign that says *Charlotte's Baby Shower*.

'Well, what do you think?'

I mean, I have to give it to her. The girl has done an amazing job. The tables are decorated with gold sequinned runners, lush white flower bouquets in the centre containing cala lilies, tulips and hydrangeas. There's gold trays of biscuits shaped like moons and stars. Above us are fluffy clouds with moons and stars falling from them.

I even seem to have my own throne. There's a giant wooden half-moon with Stay Wild Moon Child written on it in swirly black script, white and silver balloons adorning it. A wicker chair decorated with white pampas grass waits for me. Great, so all of these strangers can gawk at me

It's all so thought out and intricate. Then why do I still feel it's so impersonal? Oh that's right. Because a lot of the people here I don't even know. They must be 'Arthurs friends' or more likely James's.

Arthur rushes in rubbing the back of his neck. 'Charlotte, I'm so sorry but I have to go.'

'What?' I stare back at him, begging him with my eyes to stay.

He frowns. 'There's an emergency COBRA meeting. I'm so sorry.'

My stomach sinks. Another emergency meeting. I feel like they're every day right now. Really takes the whole *emergency* out of them.

'Okay.'

I don't sound okay. He can tell too. He looks genuinely torn, biting his lower lip, but like he always does he apologises and leaves, choosing his work over us.

His mother waves coldly from another table, surrounded by a gabble of equally posh women. The two I threw supermarket dog food on are there. *Goody.* I just need to spot some friends of my own. Where the hell is...

'Char!'

I turn with a smile to see Eloise rushing in with a present.

'Sorry I'm late, babe.' She grabs me in for a quick squeeze then takes a quick look around. 'God, alive, it looks amazing.'

'I know. I'm so glad you're here. Thank God I at least know one person here.'

She frowns. 'Aren't Sarah and Lauren coming?'

I shrug. 'No idea. I gave James my guest list, but she sorted the invites and RSVP's.'

She rolls her eyes. 'Why am I not surprised?'

'It's probably my own fault. I've been shit at keeping in touch the last few months.'

'Well, you are growing a human. I think you have a great excuse.'

James motions for us to sit down to eat. We're served a delicious three course meal, with thankfully no fish, and then everyone is left to mingle around while more champagne is served. I'm stuck with orange juice.

James drags me and my crutches over to introduce me to all of her and Arthur's friends. Some are friendly, some I can see looking at me in wonder. As if to say *'why her? Why is she so special?'* Trust me, I don't get it either.

I excuse myself to go to the toilet. I stare back at my tired puffy reflection in the mirror. You can do this, Charlotte. It's just one day. Yes, your foot is hurting, your back is aching, your armpits are rubbed raw and you feel incredibly awkward, but you can do this.

I pull my shoulders back with fake confidence and walk back out to 'my' baby shower.

I walk round the corner but stop in my tracks when I hear my name said by Arthur's mum. 'Charlotte is a sweet girl, I'm sure. And at least we know the child will be attractive.'

Her friends agree.

'We just have to hope it has its father's brains. God knows we don't want to pay for private school for it to just end up being a fairy artist like its mother.'

They all laugh as if it's hilarious. That's what I am to these women, a joke. This whole party is just some huge joke. I've never felt so humiliated. And I've shit myself in public. Twice. Air suddenly feels hard to come by. That's it, I have to get out of here.

I walk past, as quickly as I can with the damn crutches, discreetly grab my bag, and then hightail it out of there. I keep walking, scrambled thoughts rushing through my head. I'm never going to be good enough for them. Never as smart, as sophisticated. I'll always be the stupid cow that got pregnant.

I walk for what feels like hours, but must be mere

minutes, until I find myself in Whitehall Gardens. I sit down on a bench, glad for the relief, and watch as families skip past with happy smiles. I'll never have that. I've somehow got pregnant by the one man in the world that I'm completely incompatible with. I wish I'd never gone to that damn Civil Service Awards. Wish I'd never set this whole shit show in action.

But then I feel instantly bad for wishing the baby away. I clutch at my stomach.

'You're the only thing I know I want,' I say out loud. 'If only everything else was so simple.'

23

Arthur

Since Charlotte ended up in hospital I've told my PA to monitor my phone and interrupt any meetings at number ten if there's an emergency. I just can't risk not being there for her again. I try to listen as the PM waffles on, repeating himself. This whole meeting could have been done in an email.

A knock at the door startles everyone. My PA Rachel sticks her head round it, already as red as a tomato. 'I am so sorry to interrupt, but I'm afraid there's an emergency Mr Ellison needs to attend to.'

Shit.

I excuse myself, ignoring the dirty looks some give me and take my phone.

'What is it?' I ask Rachel. 'Is Charlotte okay?' I know she'll have been mortified having to interrupt that meeting.

'I just got a panicked phone call from James. Apparently Charlotte has gone missing.'

'Missing?' I repeat, more to myself. I call James back immediately. I know she'll be the calmer, rational one between her and Eloise.

'Arthur,' she answers, her voice full of concern. 'I'm worried about Charlotte. She just disappeared. We can't find her anywhere and she's not answering her phone.'

Shit.

'How the hell do you lose someone from their own baby shower?' I snap, letting days of frustration out on her.

She scoffs a laugh. 'Sorry Arthur, but I wasn't asked to babysit her. She's a grown woman who is more than capable of telling me, her host, that she's leaving. To be frank, after all the effort I've put into it I find it very rude to just leave without saying goodbye.'

I roll my eyes. Trust James to make it all about herself.

'I'm sure she had a good reason. I'll go look for her now.'

I hang up and call Eloise, aware I might get a completely different explanation.

'Hi,' she answers curtly, out of breath. It sounds like she's walking somewhere.

'What happened?' I ask, deciding to cut right to the chase.

'I don't know specifically. She went to the toilet and just never came back.'

'Did you check she's not still in there? She could be having contractions again.'

'Of course I checked. I'm out looking for her now although I have no idea where to start. She's not picking up her phone.'

'She can't have got too far. She's on bloody crutches for God's sakes.'

I practically hear her roll her eyes.

'Why do you think she left?' I press.

I know Eloise won't bullshit me.

'I think maybe she was overwhelmed. Our friends couldn't make it, so it was basically only me, James and your mum that she knew. It must be hard to have a huge party thrown in your honour but have no one you know there.'

I feel so bad. She would have coped so much better if I'd have stayed. Yet again I've let her down. I don't know how much longer I can continue to disappoint her.

'Okay. I'll come out and look too.'

I poke my head back into the meeting and state I have to leave for a family emergency. The PM is actually very understanding.

I go to the apartment first, rushing between the rooms, but she's not there. Shit. Think. Where would she go? I don't even know her favourite places. I need to talk to her more. Listen. Eloise has more chance of finding her.

Regardless I can't sit here just waiting and hoping. I walk down the street, aimlessly searching for her. Asking strangers if they've seen her, presenting a picture from my phone.

It's getting dark now and I'm worried. Why hasn't she called me back? I'm wandering down the embankment when I look over at Whitehall Gardens. I briefly remember her saying she sometimes ate lunch there when she worked for Blueberry. I wander in, passing by happy families, wondering if I'll ever be able to have that.

I search around and finally, when I'm about to give up, I spot her sitting on a bench under a tree, her crutches beside her. She's staring into space, tears streaming down her cheeks. Damn. I want to murder every single person that has made her cry. Although the biggest worry is that it's me that's caused these tears. Me that's let her down, yet again.

I take a deep breath and walk over to her. 'Charlotte?'

She looks up startled when she spots me.

'Arthur. What are you doing here?'

'I was looking for you. James and Eloise were worried when you left your baby shower.'

She scoffs. 'It sure didn't feel like *my* baby shower.'

I sit down beside her on the bench.

'Eloise mentioned that you might have felt a bit overwhelmed.'

She nods. 'I would have been okay though. I'm a big girl. But...' She stops herself.

'But what?' I press, tucking some of her hair behind her ear so I can see her beautiful face.

'Nothing.'

I lift her chin so she can't avoid me. 'Charlotte, it doesn't look like nothing. If someone has upset you, I'd like to know.'

'Well, they didn't mean to upset me.' She fiddles with her necklace. 'They didn't say it to my face anyway.'

I frown. 'So you overheard someone talking about you?'

She nods, biting her lip.

'Who?' I'm ready to murder them.

She sighs, slumping her shoulders. 'Your mother.'

Rage settles over me. I clench my fists, feeling like I'm going to explode. My fucking own mother is the one who upset the woman I... damn, I nearly just thought the woman I love. I don't love her. Do I?

'What did she say?' I ask, trying really hard not to growl.

She sniffs. 'She was saying to her friends that she hopes the baby gets your brains so it doesn't end up being a creative fairy like me.'

My mouth drops open. 'You're fucking serious?'

She shrugs. 'Why would I lie?'

I take her hand. 'Charlotte, don't for one second think I'm saying you're lying. I'm just so fucking mad right now. How dare she?'

She smiles, her eyes still glassy. 'It's fine, Arthur. She's made it no secret she doesn't care for me.'

'I don't care what she thinks. She has no fucking right.'

She stands up, with some effort. 'I suppose she's right anyway. I mean, what have I achieved anyway? I'm a bloody PA with a fashion degree I never use.'

I stand up and take her hands again. 'You've just been asked to design Alice Elizabeth Du Pont's dress. That's a huge damn deal.'

'If I don't mess it up.' She bites her lip, her brows furrowed.

I hate how her confidence has taken such a battering. She's so far from the carefree, hysterically laughing woman charming her table that I first laid my eyes on.

'Charlotte my mother has no idea what an incredible woman you are. You're caring, funny, sweet, down to earth. Everyone that knows you properly loves you and would die for you.'

'Would you?' Her eyes widen when she realises what she's said. 'Die for me, I mean,' she quickly corrects, looking down at the ground.

'Charlotte, I would use my mother as a human shield to protect you and this baby.'

She snorts a laugh. It makes my heart soar. I want to hear that laugh far more.

'I'm sure we'll never be in that particular situation. But good to know.'

I sigh, wanting to say so much more, but not sure if she'd like it.

'I would die for you Charlotte.' She looks up at me, her hazel eyes filled with what seems like hope. 'I thank God every day that this baby forced us together. Brought you into my life.'

She smiles sadly. 'It's fine, Arthur. No one is here to overhear you.'

I frown. Is she talking about our fake engagement?

'Charlotte, regardless of our fake engagement, I'm...'

'You're what?' she whispers looking longingly at me.

What's the worst that can happen if I tell her how I really feel? She could tell me she doesn't feel the same way and it will be awkward going forward. Or... well how would I feel if I didn't tell her, for fear of rejection, and she thinks I don't care. Goes and falls in love with someone else?

I take a deep breath, gulping down the racing panic.

'I'm falling in love with you.'

Her mouth drops open, her eyes widening in shock.

'Like... for real?'

'Yes, for real.' I nod. 'Now I know you might not feel the same and that's fine. I don't want you to feel any pressure to try with me, but—'

I'm stopped by her kissing me. She holds onto my face with delicate fingers, like it's a lifeline. Happiness explodes in my chest. I grab her waist and pull her in tightly, as tightly as the bump will let us. I tangle my tongue with hers, telling her everything I can't put into words. That I might already love her.

We stop when the baby kicks. We both look down at her stomach and laugh.

'I think someone is happy,' she says with a chuckle.

I smile back at her. How have I got so lucky?

'So we're really doing this?' she double checks, biting her bottom lip. 'We're trying to make it work for real.'

'Yes,' I nod. 'You're back in my bed and in my life twenty-four seven.'

She grins. 'I've never felt so happy.'

24

Saturday 12th December

Charlotte – 34 Weeks Pregnant

I've had the most amazing week. First Arthur went and professed that he's falling in love with me. I still can't believe it and find myself pinching my skin every now and then to check it's not a dream. To be able to show the affection I feel towards him in hugs and kisses is unreal. I realise now the energy it was taking out of me worrying and wondering what we were; he seems so much happier too.

Arthur Ellison is my boyfriend.

Alice Elizabeth Du Pont also came around and we discussed what kind of dress she wanted. I drew it roughly and then measured her up, all while crawling awkwardly on the floor to avoid foot pain and try to work around this giant baby. Did you know it's now the size of a pineapple? How terrifying is that?

I presented the dress to her yesterday and she was over the moon with the red A-line cocktail dress made of tulle and lace fabric. I worked my butt off to get it done in time but it was a dream to be doing something I'm passionate about.

Arthur said he's happy I'm doing something I love. I still find it amazing that he really is so interested in my happiness. How an absolute god like him has picked me when he could have anyone.

Anyway, to celebrate my first commissioned design Eloise has told me to dress up pretty and meet her for lunch at our favourite little pub in Watford. They do the best giant onion rings.

Arthur insisted on paying for a taxi to take me the full way so I didn't have to struggle on my crutches and sweat on the crowded trains. I said it wasn't necessary but I'm so glad he insisted. I'm getting up about five times a night to pee and when I am sleeping its uncomfortable, honestly, I'm absolutely exhausted.

I plaster a smile onto my face and hobble in, spotting her straight away. She waves and grabs me.

'Where are we going?'

'I booked us a private table,' she says, guiding me towards the small function room at the back.

Why the hell would she book us a private table?

She opens the door and, 'SURPRISE!' is shouted out at me.

I look around to see all of my friends; ones I've known from school, ones I made at university and still stayed in touch with, ones I'd made at Blueberry fashion house and even my mum here. Behind them are giant rose gold balloons spelling out baby.

I turn back to Eloise, still in shock, and promptly burst into tears. Everyone looks on anxiously.

'You threw me another baby shower?'

She grins. 'I did. But this one is going to actually be fun! Come on.'

Sunday 13th December

Charlotte

We had such a laugh yesterday. I finally felt like I was having a baby shower for me, and not a room of strangers. Eloise had put so much thought into it. She had photos of me and Arthur as children all around the room and played games including 'labour or porn.' Basically pictures of screaming women which we had to guess if they belonged to a woman in labour or in a porn movie. So funny. Each person brought a dish they'd made themselves, and I ate my body weight in gorgeous beige fried food. Yeah, my friends aren't the best cooks.

Arthur even surprised me by turning up an hour before the end to chat to everyone and pose for photos.

Arthur walks into the bedroom, wet and delicious from a shower, in only his towel. My god, do I want to lick him dry.

'Have you seen this?' He hands me over a newspaper and turns it to the celebrity section.

There in a big image is Alice Elizabeth Du Pont in my dress.

'Oh my God!' I shriek, jumping up and down on my bum. 'My dress! It's my dress!'

He grins back at me. 'I know. Your first official write up.'

I quickly read over the small description.

'Alice Elizabeth Du Pont wears a dress designed by Cabinet Secretary Arthur Ellison's fiancé Charlotte Bellswain.'

'Oh my god they mentioned me! How amazing!' I let the feeling of euphoria wash over me. 'Do you actually think I could make a business out of this?'

He smiles. 'Of course I do.'

Wow.

'Perfect time for me to give you this.' He hands over a silver case. Inside are the most stunning gold embossed business cards.

Charlotte Bellswain.

Bespoke Fashion Designer

'I love them.' It's then I realise he must have ordered these before the story was printed. 'Wait, you had the faith in me to order these?'

He scoffs. 'Charlotte, I ordered these as soon as you told me you were pregnant. I know that you can do great things. You've just needed the chance.'

I stare back at him, open mouthed, no doubt like an unattractive fish.

'I can't believe you did that.'

He shrugs, as if he isn't the wonderful human being he is. 'I'll show you the dated invoice if you like?'

I shake my head, feeling myself blush. How is this guy so into me? I still don't get it.

'So you had a good day yesterday?' he asks, sitting down on the bed and tucking a bit of my hair behind my ear. I love when he does that. It makes me feel cherished.

'Yeah.' I smile. 'I know it sounds bad, but it was nice to be with my own crowd.'

He smiles sadly and I know what he's thinking. He

wishes I got on better with James and his mother. I sent James a quick sorry message after I'd ran out of the shower and thanked her for organising it for me. Arthur apparently also spoke to his mother and warned her to back off or we'd be out of her life forever.

I do still worry that we're from such different worlds. I'll never fit into his and he'll never fit into mine. But for now, I choose to ignore all of my niggling doubts and be happy.

25

Wednesday 16th December

Charlotte - 35 Weeks Pregnant

I've had no less than fifteen women call me since the article about my dress. After my initial excitement I sat down and really thought about what I want. Turns out I don't want to jump headfirst into a new business this close to delivering the baby. With my bleeding and early contractions there's a chance the baby could be premature. Plus, I'm still on these bastard crutches. My life is hard enough right now. It's the last thing I need.

So I've decided I want to relax and finally sort out the nursery. Get in the right head space. God knows I'm not sleeping at night anymore. I find it easier to take small naps during the day. I bravely told the women this. I braced myself, expecting them to lose interest immediately, but instead they asked me to call them when the baby is born and I've got childcare sorted.

I have however decided I'm going to design my own dress for Arthur's mum's Christmas Eve party. I've had a look online and I can't find anything I like that will fit me, but I already have some amazing ideas. I just have to see if I can get the fabric I need in time.

It also gives me the opportunity to return a lot of the presents I got at James' baby shower. I mean talk about ridiculous; a sterling silver egg cup, some baby clothes from his mum that look like they come from the Edwardian times and a baby monitor that I already bought for myself. After that I plan on buying some bits for the nursery.

I thought this was all a good idea until I remembered I'm on crutches and holding a bag full of returns while also attempting to walk with them is hard damn work. Maybe I'll skip the nursery bits.

I'm already sweating my tits off as I queue up in John Lewis, knowing all of the stuff is from here. It's finally my turn and I step forward with what I hope it a friendly smile.

'Hi, I think a few of these things are from here and I want to return them, but I don't have the receipt. Can I get store credit?'

I hope he'll take pity on the pregnant girl with the crutches. Damn, there needs to be some advantages to this.

'I can look into that for you, madam.'

'Charlotte?' Someone calls from behind me.

I swing round to see James walking straight towards me, three gowns over her arm. Shit. I don't want to be caught returning the stuff and have her think I'm ungrateful.

I turn back to the woman, hoping she's going to put the returned items away and quickly. She's still talking to her manager on the phone.

'What are you doing here?' James asks me, already by me. Those damn gazelle-like legs.

I try to stand in front of the items so she can't see.

'Oh, just um...'

'Madam,' the cashier interrupts, 'we *can* give you store credit.'

James' face falls as she takes in the items I'm returning.

'Oh, that's bits from the baby shower. You didn't like them?' She actually looks crestfallen.

'Um... I'm just... really particular,' I quickly bullshit. 'But all the stuff was great, just not my style.'

She looks over the baby clothes. 'I helped Linda pick these out for you. You know a lot of time went into buying this for you. I don't think she'll be very pleased.'

Is she threatening to tell her? Any previous sympathy for upsetting her has gone.

'Well, hopefully we can keep this between the two of us. Right?' I smile with hope, eyes pleading desperately.

She quirks her lip as if she can smell bad fish. 'I suppose.'

There's an awkward beat of silence where neither of us know where to look. God, I despise the tension.

'Anyway, must be off. See you on Christmas Eve.'

Saturday 19th December

Charlotte

Arthur hasn't mentioned James catching me returning the baby stuff, thank God

To make matters worse when I got home I found a card in the post from her. She'd taken it upon herself to send out thank you cards for my baby shower. *So sweet of her* Arthur said. Yeah right. She chose a picture she'd taken of me to be plastered on the front. I look extremely fat, my double chin on full view and I look slightly shocked, as if she caught me off guard.

He has no idea this is her way of declaring war. Well bring it on bitch. Arthur is mine and there is no way I'm giving him up for anyone, especially her.

The stuff I really wanted was from Ikea so I got a delivery. Arthur kept asking me to look at other higher end websites, which I did, but I found identical stuff for three times the price. I don't want to waste money like that. Especially when it'll likely be covered in baby vomit soon.

Arthur drags the huge cardboard boxes into the nursery.

'Thanks. Now all we need to do is put it together.'

He sighs, looking hassled. 'Can't we just pay someone to do it?'

I laugh. 'Where's the fun in that?'

Frowning he scratches his neck. 'I don't see there being any fun in my near future.'

His phone pings several times with incoming emails.

'Come on,' I encourage with what I hope is a sexy smile. 'It won't take long if we work together.'

AN HOUR later we're both stressed to fuck. Yeah, I only ever thought Ikea furniture was fun because either my dad or Josh put it together for me. Arthur might be great at his job, but his strong point isn't putting flat packs together.

'Where's the plastic thing?' he asks irritably.

'What plastic thing?'

'The thing that holds this part up?' His face is tight with anxiety.

I look at the instructions trying to gauge what the hell he's talking about.

'You shouldn't need a plastic part. You should need one of those little wooden bits.'

'Ugh, this is bullshit,' he complains, letting the piece he's been holding up fall with a loud clatter. 'None of it makes fucking sense!'

I snort a laugh. 'Well I suppose it is a Swedish company. But the instructions are in English.'

His phone is constantly binging in the background. Every time it does I see him looking longingly towards it.

'Whatever Charlotte, I'm done with this.' He stands up, clenching his jaw. 'I have work to do, far more important stuff. Just hire someone to put it together.'

He walks out, no doubt to retrieve his precious phone.

I look around at the parts of wood. Where's the sweet day I had planned where we'd lovingly put our babies' room together? The cold hard truth is that he just doesn't care enough. I look down at my bump, a tear falling down my cheek. We're not enough for him.

I pull myself together and decide I need some fresh air. I grab my crutches and walk out into the living room where he's already deep in work on his laptop, grab my coat and slam the door childishly behind me. I call Eloise as soon as I'm on the street.

'He just doesn't care,' I wail down the line to her, crying so hard I create snot bubbles. Real attractive, Charlotte.

'Okay babe, but can I be real here?' she asks.

'Of course.'

She sighs. 'Babe this is flat pack furniture. No man likes putting it together. No man likes going to Ikea. You, by some miracle found Josh who loved it as much as you, but that's why I always thought he was gay.'

I roll my eyes even though she can't see me. He wore a pink shirt once and she basically booked his ticket for gay pride.

'I just... I guess I don't feel like a priority.'

'Babe it's obvious to me that Arthur is head over heels in love with you. You're just over-reacting because of the baby hormones, which frankly are turning you into a complete weirdo.'

'I mean, you're right there.' We both laugh. I need the break it brings.

'Don't you remember the day me and Stuart broke up? It was the day we were putting our flat pack together. It's a breaking point for a lot of couples. And Arthur said he'll pay for someone to put it together, so what's the big deal?'

I know she's right. I'm just feeling strange and insecure. Which I shouldn't be. Arthur has told me he's falling in love with me. He hasn't voiced any other doubts.

'Thanks, El, you have made me feel better. There's still no way I can convince you to come to Arthur's mum's Christmas Eve party?'

She snorts a laugh. 'No chance in hell. But have fun!'

26

Thursday 24th December

Charlotte - 36 Weeks Pregnant

'Thank you again for coming,' Arthur says to me as we rock slowly from side to side on the moodily lit black and white dance floor.

His mum has hired an entire hotel in Knightsbridge and still gone to town decorating as if it's a blank canvas. The hotel itself is so grand, all high ceilings and gold but she's added red and white balloons complete with candy canes. There are snowy garlands, a hot chocolate bar off to the side with sweets labelled as *'Santa's cookies'*, *'elf treats'* and *'reindeer noses'*, plus fairy lights on every surface. I have to give it to her, its magical. I think our future child will love these parties.

We're all in matching red and white too, as per her request. Well, except I had to be a bit rebellious. My empire line dress is silver. It's the only shape that makes me look slightly less huge and the silver made me feel pretty. Anything that makes me feel less of a swollen pregnant woman right now has to be allowed. My ankles are now puffy too. I've also sprayed painted my crutches silver so I feel a bit more chic.

Apparently all money raised is going to a children's cancer charity. I suppose she must have some goodness in her to do that. Either that or she just wants everyone to *think* she's charitable

His mum taps me on the shoulder as we do our strange stationary dance. I turn, eyes wide to face her. God, what does she want with me? Just when I was enjoying myself.

'Charlotte, can I please have a word?' she wrings her hands in front of her. Is she feeling awkward?

It's the first time I've seen any real emotion come from her. I look back to Arthur who smiles. I have to try, for him.

'Okay. Sure.'

She helps me with my crutches and guides me in between waiters serving canapes, over to a quieter corner where she directs me towards a chair.

She swallows. 'Charlotte, I want to apologise for what I said at your baby shower.'

I fold my arms defensively across my chest. I want more of an apology than that. The woman was bad mouthing me at my own shower.

'And for how I've generally treated you since you've come into my life. I must admit I've found it hard to accept you and the baby. It was all so sudden. Such a shock to me. Truth be told, I was always expecting him to marry James.'

I roll my eyes. I think *everyone* expected that.

'It still doesn't excuse your rudeness,' I say calmly. I want to get my point across without bursting into tears.

She nods, pressing her lips together. 'I know. I'm repulsed by my actions and I hope we can start again. Arthur said you're having real success in the fashion world. I want to be in yours and my grandchild's life and to help support you in any way I can.'

I nod. Arthur has obviously scared her into submission. The truth is that I'd like her to be in the baby's life. God knows with Arthur's job I'm going to need all the help I can get.

'I have no problem with that. All I ask is that you treat us both with kindness and not talk about us behind our back.'

She nods sincerely. 'I promise, Charlotte. It's my New Year's resolution and unlike other people I always keep mine.'

I shrug. 'Then fine. You're forgiven.'

She smiles and I realise it's the first real one I've had from her. It fully reaches her eyes and her crow's feet wrinkle. 'Arthur was right. You are a lovely person. Thank you so much for accepting my apology.'

'You're welcome. Now I'm going to go and find Arthur.'

I look around but he's no longer on the dance floor. He's not at the bar either. I can't see him anywhere. That's weird.

Arthur

Charlotte's barely gone off with Mum when James appears wearing a dress that shows off far too much cleavage.

She smiles devilishly. 'Arthur, can I have a private word please?'

I frown but follow her, seen as she's already started walking. She walks out of the room, down a corridor and into a small office by the toilets. I'm sure we're not allowed to be in here.

'What's up?' I ask, hands in my pockets

The more time I spend with Charlotte the less I want to spend with James. How did I never realise how self-indulged and judgemental she is?

'I want to... I want to...' she stops again, wavering.

I roll my eyes, quickly losing patience with her. 'Jesus, James, spit it out.'

She clears her throat. 'I want you to know that there are more options for you.'

I frown back at her. What the hell is she going on about?

'What do you mean? Options?'

She swallows. 'What I mean is, don't feel you have to marry Charlotte just because you got her pregnant. I know you're worried about your reputation, but there are plenty of blended families in the world now. It's not as terrible as it once was.'

I shake my head in disbelief. Where the hell is this coming from?

'Sorry, are you telling me I shouldn't be marrying Charlotte?'

She sighs, leaning on a chair. 'I just don't think she's right for you, Artie.'

Like she fucking knows. 'Charlotte is everything I need. She's sweet, loving; loyal.'

She scoffs and mutters. 'Loyal,' under her breath.

'Sorry? What the hell do you mean by that?'

She's seriously pissing me off.

She takes out her phone and scrolls through, handing it over to me. On it are pictures of Charlotte out with a man. Having dinner with him all dressed up. Having what looks like a coffee date with him. I look back at her expecting an explanation.

'I know you'll be mad.' She pauses to bite her lip. 'But for your own protection I had her followed.'

'You hired a fucking private investigator?'

Of course she did; James trusts no one.

'I did,' she nods. 'And aren't you glad I did. That man in the photos is her ex-boyfriend Joshua Moore. Tell me, Artie, did she share this bit of information with you?'

My stomach drops. I mean she's right, she hasn't told me. Why the hell hasn't she? Especially if its innocent, which I assume it would be. Charlotte's not like that.

'She's been leading you on, while all the time keeping a backup option viable. Joshua and her only broke up because she didn't want to settle down. And now that she's ready she's eyeing up her opportunity to get him back.'

'No,' I say out loud, shaking my head. I can't believe this. I refuse to believe this.

She locks eyes with mine. 'Pictures don't lie, Artie. I wanted so desperately for you to have found your happiness, but I don't want you to rush into something that isn't right.'

I mean, could she just be looking out for my best interest? Is it possible?

'Maybe you're right,' I muse aloud. Could I have been living a fantasy the last couple of months, ignoring any warning signs?

She nods with a sad smile. 'You know I am. It's definitely not as simple as you're making out. Pretending to play families with this absolute stranger of a woman. I still can't believe you moved her in so quickly.'

Ugh, she sounds just like my mother. I want to get away from her poisonous words.

'What choice did I have?' I snap back. 'Let her leave and move to Devon? Never see my baby again?'

She scoffs. 'That's if the baby's even yours.'

She's on thin fucking ice right now. I can't even talk I'm so mad.

'I do think you should have a paternity test once the baby is born.'

She won't believe anything good in Charlotte. The quickest way to escape is to have her think I believe her. That way I can get back to Charlotte and ask her about the Joshua thing. I'm sure there's a reasonable explanation.

'Hmm. Maybe I should,' I say.

'I think it's the right thing to do,' she nods in agreement. 'But obviously don't spook Charlotte now. Keep up appearances until the baby is born and then we can secretly get the test done.'

I nod, feeling like the life has been kicked out of me. How can she believe Charlotte would be so vindictive? How have I been so blind to this behaviour before now?

'Okay.'

She smiles sadly at me. 'Oh, Artie. Come here.'

She presses herself against me. It doesn't feel right. Not without Charlotte's bump. Not without Charlotte's sweet scent of flowers.

'Well at least you have some sense,' she adds.

People seem a lot happier when I agree to a DNA test. My mum has been insisting on one since the beginning. But I know Charlotte and I know she wouldn't lie to me. She's not impressed by fancy expensive things. She just wants a simple life. Definitely not the type to trap a person with a baby. There must be a reason why she was with her ex-boyfriend.

She leans back, looking up at me.

'You have more options, Arthur,' she whispers.

She edges towards me. Shit, is she trying to kiss me? I

jump back in revulsion, pushing her away. Her eyes widen in vulnerability.

'What are you doing?' I ask, unable to hide the shock.

'I'm an option, Arthur,' she purrs, looking at my lips.

'You?' I repeat in disbelief. Is she fucking serious? How deluded can you get?

'I think I've waited for you long enough. You always said you didn't want children, so I waited for you. Now you've changed your mind and that's okay. It might be too late for us to have them, but we can share this baby with Charlotte. We can be together.' She steps forward and strokes my cheek.

'No, James,' I whisper, taking her hand and removing it. 'I had no idea you felt like this. Why didn't you tell me?'

She pushes my hand off. 'Because I felt we had time. I was happy for you to put your career first. I still am. But I think you know that we're better suited.'

I stand back. 'Maybe on paper, James. But I love Charlotte.'

And shit, I do. Forget this falling bullshit. I'm in love with Charlotte. I've been lying to myself about it for weeks.

She shakes my head. 'You don't. You just think that because of the baby.'

I shake my head. I need to be clear here. Let her know there's no chance for us.

'James, even if Charlotte and the baby didn't exist. Me and you would never work. I'm sorry but I just don't feel like that about you.'

Her face falls. 'Oh. Oh dear.'

She suddenly looks smaller, her shoulders hunched, her eyes filled with tears. I feel sorry for her. Especially if she feels I've been leading her on.

I take her hand in mine. 'I'll always love you as a friend, James. But we'll never be anything more.'

She nods, a tear falling down her cheek.

'I'm sorry, but I'm going to find Charlotte.'

Charlotte

I can't see him anywhere so decide to escape to the bathroom. Of course I need another wee. I can waste some time in there, maybe even give Eloise a call and see how her evening is going. I'd far rather be at Lauren's house party in Watford.

I walk down the long corridor to the toilets that I've already visited several times tonight, but stop when I hear Arthur's voice.

I creep quietly towards the door and listen in.

'Pictures don't lie, Arthur,' James says. 'I wanted so desperately for you to have found your happiness, but I don't want you to rush into something that isn't right.'

The absolute bitch. I knew she hated me.

'Maybe you're right,' Arthur says.

No, she's not right, Arthur. She's a massive bitch. Don't listen to her.

'You know I am. It's definitely not as simple as you're making out,' she says. 'Pretending to play families with this absolute stranger of a woman. I still can't believe you moved her in so quickly.'

'What choice did I have?' He snaps back.

My spine tingles at the change in his tone. I don't know this Arthur.

'Let her leave and move to Devon? Never see my baby again.'

I feel sick. He doesn't want me. Of course he doesn't. He just wants the baby. It's all been a lie.

'That's if the baby's even yours.'

I wait for him to stand up for me. To shout at her for the accusation of me being a slut.

But there's too much silence.

'I do think you should get a paternity test once the baby is born.'

My stomach bottoms out.

'Hmm. Maybe I should.'

Oh my god. He believes her. He thinks he needs a DNA test? I can't breathe. It's like all of the air has been sucked from my lungs.

'I think it's the right thing to do. But obviously don't spook Charlotte now. Keep up appearances until the baby is born and then we can secretly get the test done.'

I gasp, quickly covering my mouth with my hand.

'Okay.'

I can't believe it. They've been colluding together from the start. It's all been an act. I've been so unbelievably stupid.

I turn and walk away, unable to hear any more without being violently sick. I head for the exit, a million thoughts racing through my mind.

My world is falling apart around me. He wants a DNA test. How can he believe the baby might not be his, that he still has that seed of doubt? He doesn't know me well, at all. I don't know him well. We're basically strangers thrust together by one night of passion.

I might have fallen head over heels in love with him, but to him we'll always just be a situation. Something to be handled. There's no way he would have given me a second thought otherwise. He's been pretending, telling me what I need to hear in order to keep me close. All the time planning a happily ever after with James.

I leave, rushing back to the flat. I pack my suitcase, tears running down my cheeks. I don't care what I'm packing as I throw clothes haphazardly in along with my toiletries, I just need to get out of here.

Arthur

I head straight to the main hall as soon as I can get away from James. I can't seem to find Charlotte in the crowd. After the shit show with James, I need to feel her in my arms. Need to be reminded that there are good people in the world.

I spot Mum from across the room. I walk quickly over there.

'Mum, how was your chat with Charlotte?'

She smiles. 'Good. She's forgiven me. You were right. She really is a good woman. Hold onto her.'

'I intend to. Did you see where she went off to?'

'No, I think she was looking for you.' She frowns back at me. 'I assumed she'd found you.'

'No.' I'm already walking away. 'Thanks,' I shout back as an afterthought.

I speak to one of the doormen and ask if he's seen an eight-month pregnant woman on crutches leave. Kind of easy to spot.

'Yeah, she left a little while ago. Seemed to be upset about something.'

The thought of her miserable makes my own heart ache. Wait a minute. Mum said she was looking for me. Left upset. Shit, what if she found me and overheard me and James? Got the wrong end of the stick?

I race towards the flat, not even stopping to call a cab. If she heard all that she's going to think all manner of unreasonable awful things about me.

I finally reach the door, sweaty and out of breath. I open it to an eerie silence. My stomach rolls, a chill spreading throughout my body, finding its place in my heart. She's gone. I know it even before I run through the rooms, hands in my hair in desperation. Her suitcase is gone and most of her wardrobe is empty. My Grandma's ring is on the breakfast bar.

Shit. I lean against the wall, needing something to support my jellied legs. I take my phone out and slide to the floor, as I press call. It goes straight to answerphone. Double shit.

'Charlotte, it's me. I think you've got the wrong idea. Please call me back so I can explain.'

Happy revellers in the street below shout out, excited for Christmas. I start Christmas alone, as I've always been. Except now that I've had the taste of love I don't intend to let it go. Charlotte isn't going to run that easily.

27

Monday 28th December

Arthur

*I*t's been four days and she still hasn't called me back. I've left about twenty voicemails and thirty text messages begging her to listen to me.

I spent Christmas alone in the flat pigging out on takeaways. I haven't even bothered to shave the last few days. I'm too depressed now that my very reason for living has gone without a trace. Without her nothing feels right. I miss her so much it hurts deep within my chest.

I'd planned to try and have some time off in between Christmas and New Year, but now there's no point so I'm back at Whitehall. Could I really have screwed up the best thing to ever happen to me? I know that if I could just see her face to face I could explain. Get her to understand. To come back. To maybe even consider falling in love with me half as hard as I have her.

I've tried calling Eloise too but she won't take my calls, and I'm not sure if she's due in before the New Year. I'm just back from grabbing a sandwich my PA insisted I buy when I spot Eloise in the office. Her eyes widen when she sees me. I make a beeline from her as she turns and tries to hurry away.

'Eloise, I need to talk to you urgently,' I demand, hand already on her elbow, pulling her to face me.

She turns on a huff, crossing her arms across her chest. 'What do you want, Arthur?'

I know her attitude is just because her best friend is in pain. Pain she thinks I caused. That doesn't stop people looking over, wondering how she can be so rude to me.

'I want to know where Charlotte and my baby are?'

She scoffs. 'Oh, but you can't be so sure it's yours until you get the DNA test.'

Shit. She did hear the worst part of that conversation. It must have sounded abhorrent to her. I'll kill James.

'Look, she misunderstood. It was taken out of context.'

She rolls her eyes. 'Said like a true politician.'

'Eloise, please,' I beg, attempting to communicate how desperate I am.

'No, Arthur. You've made your bed, now I suggest you lie in it. Alone.'

Charlotte – 37 Weeks Pregnant

I'm so glad I came home for Christmas. Not that I expected to find my divorced parents in bed together. Apparently they're back on. Most kids would be over the moon that their parents were giving it another go. Not me. It just means a whole lot of more drama between the two of them. Yeah they're happy now, but it's only a matter of time before they're at each other's throats again. This must be the sixth time they're *trying again.*

To be fair they've been absolute angels since I arrived crying hysterically and standing in their bedroom doorway. In fact Mum's been treating me like I've been in a car crash. Feeding me biscuits, wrapping me in a blanket, insisting I need more sugar for the shock. It's a wonder I wasn't a podgy kid what with my mum being such a feeder.

And without my pride stopping me from asking Arthur for help, it's so much easier to have someone to assist with showering and life necessities, and generally do everything for me.

I've told them everything. Dad looked like he wanted to murder Arthur but I begged him to let me handle it. I suppose it'll all have to be done through the courts now. Or mediators at best.

I don't want it to get nasty and to cost us both a fortune, yet I also know that I can't ever see him again. He makes me weak. Makes me believe in fairy tales that aren't possible. I need to be strong now, for me and the baby.

I get a text from Eloise to say he's been pestering her at work for my parent's address. She didn't give it, thank God. Says he looks rough, like he hasn't slept.

The sadistic part of me is glad. Good, he should feel bad for what he's done. Not that I've done this to punish him. I've actually done this for the baby. Being that distressed isn't good for me or it. I've only been here a few days, but already I feel cared for and the sea breeze is helping me to sleep better. I might just stay here after all.

Regardless of the situation—God I hate that phrase— but regardless of the situation, I won't stop him from seeing the baby. He can have supervised visits with someone else present while I'm still breastfeeding and then when its older it can go to him every second weekend. Just like normal split up parents. Most of them were together longer than one night before conceiving mind.

Oh well. This is my life now and I choose to embrace it. No matter how hard I cry into my pillow every night.

Thursday 31st December

Arthur

I've broken all of the rules and bribed Gerry in HR to give me Charlotte's previous address. There is no way I'm starting next year without her. I knock three times that very evening at a house in Watford, determined to find out where she is.

A young woman with a nose ring answers the door. 'Yes?'

'Hi. I'm Arthur Ellison. I'm Charlotte's...' I stop, realising I don't know what I am to her. 'Can I please come in? It's extremely urgent.'

She rolls her eyes but begrudgingly lets me in. Other women are setting up balloons and streamers, obviously planning a New Year's Eve party.

'I need to know her parent's address in Devon.'

'Why?' she asks, staring at me suspiciously.

'Because she's got the wrong end of the stick of something I said. She's run off to her parents and it is imperative that I speak with her.'

She huffs but goes into the kitchen drawer. Loads of

loose papers are in there, shuffled around. God they live like pigs. Charlotte must have hated living here.

'Here it is,' she says, handing over the address written in Charlotte's handwriting. 'She gave it to forward her mail onto. Well, before she moved in with you.'

I snatch it off her before she can change her mind.

'Thank you so much.'

Looks like I'm driving to Devon.

I leave, but just as I'm closing the gate I see Joshua Moore coming this way. I recognise him from the photos Eloise showed me.

'What the hell are you doing here?' I ask, wanting to kill him.

'I wanted to see if Charlotte was here. I haven't been able to contact her and I'm worried. I thought she might come back here.'

'You shouldn't be looking for her,' I snap, anger surging through my veins. 'She's none of your business.'

'Why are *you* here?' he asks, narrowing his eyes. 'Oh, I see. You're the reason I haven't been able to contact her. It's because you've upset her, haven't you?'

'Like I said,' I growl, clenching my fists. 'It's none of your fucking business. Leave her the fuck alone.'

'You don't deserve her,' he snaps, his face scrunched up in distaste.

Don't I know it.

'I still love her,' he continues, 'and I'll marry her tomorrow if she'll have me.'

'Well she won't,' I bark back, unsure if that's true.

Maybe she would be happier with him. If I love her I should want her to be happy regardless.

He sighs, his shoulders slouching. 'I know. The sad truth is that woman loves you. She only ever talked about you.

Please don't fuck up your chance. Or I *will* try and take her from you.'

Well, fuck. I actually like the guy.

'I don't intend to.'

Charlotte

Mum and Dad wanted me to stay up to ring the New Year in with them. I can't face it so have gone to bed instead. I just want to bury my head under the duvet and ignore the fact that I'm going into the New Year as a single mum.

I've almost drifted off when the sounds of a car pulling up, and someone walking on the gravel wakes me up. I hear a knock on the door. Who the hell could that be at gone half eleven? It can't be Arthur. He doesn't know where I am. I listen to my dad talking to someone. Is that? No, it couldn't be.

I grab my crutches and hop to the top of the stairs and listen in. The baby starts kicking, as if knowing daddy is here.

'Now listen here, son,' Dad warns. 'I don't care how long you've travelled, she doesn't want to see you. Especially at this hour.'

'Please,' he pleads. God, just hearing his voice. The desperation in it. I can't bear it.

I sit on my bum and shuffle a few steps down. 'It's fine, Dad. Let him in.'

I shuffle the last remaining steps, finally coming into view.

He looks far worse than how Eloise described him. He's unshaved, his eyes seem hollow, haunted. He definitely hasn't slept properly since I've left.

I should be pleased but instead I want nothing more

than to go to him, to wrap my arms around him and reassure him everything will be okay. But I can't. Or I shouldn't. I need to put myself and the baby first.

He gives me his hand to help me up.

'Hi,' he says sheepishly. 'Can we please talk?'

Mum bursts into the hall carrying a glass of champagne. 'Who is it, Phil?' Her eyes widen when she spots Arthur. 'Oh, Jesus.'

'It's okay, Mum.' I look to him. 'Let's go in here.' I point towards the kitchen and let him help me sit down at the table, hoping Mum and Dad haven't got their ears pressed up to the door.

He looks around and I remember that such quaint surroundings must be weird to him. Us regular people don't have butlers like Downton Abbey. Rich idiot.

He swallows, clearly nervous. He should be. I'm still furious.

He takes a quick deep breath. 'I'm so sorry for what I'm assuming you overheard, Charlotte. But if you'd stuck around you would have heard me sticking up for you. Telling James that I'm not interested in her and never will be.'

He said that? Well yeah I'd have liked to have heard that. But how can I trust anything that comes out of his mouth anymore? James told him to play along. To keep me sweet.

I glare at him. 'You told her you were getting a DNA test. What part of that is sticking up for me?'

He sighs, his shoulders drooping over. 'I just said that I'd think about it to shut her up. I wanted to get out of there as quickly as possible. And well... she'd just shown me you'd been meeting up with your ex-boyfriend. I didn't know what to think.'

Damn, I didn't know he'd found out about that. It obviously doesn't look good me seeing Joshua.

'Look I just went out with Josh once as friends and the other time I bumped into him at the cafe. I spent most of the time talking about you.'

'I know. He told me.'

Since when did they meet up?

'He also told me he's still in love with you.'

Bless Josh.

'Well, I'm not in love with him.'

'What did you tell him about me?' he asks, eyeing the bump.

I sigh. 'Honestly? I told him how I wasn't sure we were going to work. That we're so different.'

He smiles sadly, a line forming between his brows.

'But I never once considered leaving you to go to him. I've just found this whole relying on someone thing hard to handle. I'm used to being let down. And guess what, I was.'

'I'm so sorry, Charlotte.' He leans forward and takes my hands.

'Anyway, it doesn't matter.' I shrug, as if unbothered. 'I'm not going to stop you seeing the baby.' I take my hands back. 'I'll call you when I'm in labour and we can sort a schedule.'

His jaw clenches. 'I don't want a mother fucking schedule, Charlotte. I want you.'

I gasp. 'Huh?'

He stands and comes round to my side, kneeling in front of me.

'When are you going to get it into your stupid head? I don't just want the baby. I want you.'

'But... why? I don't get it. You want a DNA test. You're just trying to keep me sweet until the baby is born.'

He shakes his head, taking my hands again. 'I don't need

LAURA BARNARD

a DNA test. Charlotte, I've fallen in love with you. I didn't even realise it until you'd gone. I'm useless without you.'

I sigh. 'You can't just be with someone because they make your life easier.'

He scoffs a laugh. 'You think you make my life easier? Every second of every day I'm distracted by you. Wondering if you've eaten, if you've drunk enough, if you'll be satisfied being stuck with me forever.'

'Why wouldn't I be?'

He looks down at the floor. 'Because Joshua is right. I don't deserve you.'

My heart breaks for him. My screwed-up Arthur.

'Not many people would accept a partner that isn't theirs ninety percent of the time,' he adds. 'I fear you'll resent me even more when the baby is born. If you're under some illusion that I'll work less when it's here, I'm sorry to say that won't be true. And I already hate myself because of it.'

'I know,' I curve my lips, cupping his cheek with my palm. 'But as you say, we're in this situation now and we have to make the best of it. But I don't want to end up like my parents, screaming at each other in front of our child.'

He smiles sadly. 'We're not your parents, Charlotte. I can't promise you we'll never argue, but don't you think it's worth the risk? Do you... do you think you could forgive me? Trust me again? Learn to love me one day?'

I look down into his vulnerable eyes, a tear escaping my own.

'You idiot. I'm already madly in love with you. I just didn't want to waste my life hoping you would one day feel the same.'

He laughs. 'Really?'

'Of course. What's not to love?' We both chuckle a laugh.

'The real question is if you really think you love me? I don't want you confused because of the baby.'

He smiles at me. His secret smile I've missed so dearly.

'Charlotte I love you for so many more reasons than you growing my baby in your tummy. You're sweet, unjaded, funny, caring. Everything that I've never known. I can't wait for us to start our family, no matter how unconventional it is. If that means me commuting to Devon on the weekends, so be it.'

'Okay,' I smile, feeling more confident. 'So we agree, truthful from now on? We're together and fuck everyone else?'

He grins and I see a glimpse of my normal cocky Arthur Ellison.

'Agreed.'

He leans forward and pecks a quick kiss on my lips and then the bump.

'I just have one more question to ask you,' he says, chewing on his lip.

'What's that?'

He pulls something out of his pocket. I see it's his Grandma's engagement ring.

'I told you before that my grandma told me to give this to the woman I marry. What I didn't tell you is that she also said it had to be the woman I loved like no other.'

My heart starts thumping in my chest.

'You're that woman. Charlotte Bellswain, will you marry me, for real?'

I chuckle as tears stream down my face.

'Of course I will.'

I jump into his arms as my mum and dad burst into the room congratulating us. Clearly listening then.

'Just in time for New Year,' Mum says, excitedly looking at her watch. 'Ten, nine, eight...'

Dad joins in counting down.

Arthur pulls me close. 'We're starting the new year as we mean to go on. Together.'

He pulls me in and kisses me while fireworks go off in the distance and Mum and Dad shout out *happy New Year*.

EPILOGUE – THREE YEARS LATER

Charlotte

 *W*e're moving into our new house today. Finally free of this apartment. Let me tell you, having a three-year-old with no garden is a nightmare. This flat was never built for a family. The minute I gave birth I knew we'd have to eventually move.

Ophelia Elizabeth Bellswain Ellison was born on the 19th January weighing a whopping nine pounds two. She looked just like a mini Arthur and still does. My hazel eyes with Arthur's mop of dark curls. Eloise visited us in hospital and joked she was glad she didn't come out black. That then they'd really have wanted a DNA test. I'm glad we can laugh about it now.

She's the most amazing child. She seems to have my creative side, always drawing and designing dresses, but is also super smart like Arthur. Truth be told it makes for an exhausting three-nager. She questions everything and always wants to learn more. The only break I get is when she goes to Nanny Linda's while I design dresses. She really is the best Grandma. She dotes on that little girl.

My business really took off. Another reason why we need a bigger place. I'm going to have my own sewing room so I can lock it all away from Ophelia.

I actually have a big meeting with a department store next week to discuss giving me my own six-piece line in shops. I'm cautious because if it's going to have my name on it I want it to be of the best quality. I don't want to compromise on that.

Arthur still works crazy hours as Cabinet Secretary, but he's got more precious with his time. He now has two phones. Only three people at work have his personal number so he often turns off his work phone and is only interrupted for proper emergencies. It means the short time we have together is quality time.

He's the most amazing dad. He really indulges Ophelia's questions and informs me that she'll need to be well educated if she's to become prime minister. Dream on. I'd rather her be a yoga instructor. Sounds far less stressful.

James married a stockbroker a year after Ophelia was born. We still hear about her and wish her well, but we don't have a relationship anymore.

Arthur lugs the last of the boxes into the kitchen.

'Now that we've moved will you ever set a date for the wedding?' he asks.

I grin back at him. 'I love it when you're all needy.'

He chuckles a laugh. 'I just don't think I can carry on much longer not being married to you.'

I wrap my arms around him. 'Maybe this summer?' I suggest

He grins, eyes alight. 'We're sitting down with the diary tonight.'

'Oh, Mr Ellison. Always so bossy.'

THE END

ALSO BY LAURA BARNARD

The Debt & the Doormat Series

The Debt & the Doormat

The Baby & the Bride

Porn Money & Wannabe Mummy

One Month Til I do Series

Adventurous Proposal

Marrying Mr Valentine

Babes of Brighton Series

Excess Baggage

Love Uncovered

Bagging Alice

Standalones

Tequila and Tea Bags

Give it Arrest

Once Upon a Wish-Mas

Cock and Bull

Road Trip (co written with Andie M Long)

Heath, Cliffs & Wandering Hearts (Young Adult)

ABOUT THE AUTHOR

Amazon Bestselling author Laura Barnard writes British quirky laugh out loud romantic comedy.

She lives in Hertfordshire, UK, with her husband and daughter.

In her spare time she enjoys drinking her body weight in tea, cuddling dogs, setting her friends up together (very successfully), indulging in the power nap and reading past her bedtime.

Sign up to her Newsletter HERE

ACKNOWLEDGMENTS

Thank you so much for picking up my book - I would love you forever if you took a moment to leave a review on Amazon / Goodreads.

Big thanks to Robert Cheesewright, a civil servant for ten years, he was my fountain of knowledge. Without him there I would have had no idea!

Thanks to Sandra from Two Book Pushers for telling me her hilarious pregnancy story which made it into the book.

Thanks to all of the mamas that shared their pregnancy stories - us women really do go through so much to make these beautiful babies.

To my personal cheerleaders; the hubster, Mumma L, Auntie Mad and Betty. Your unfailing faith in me is what keeps me going.

I am also so appreciative for all of the people that constantly take time out of their day to promote me, whether it be bloggers, bookstagrammers or readers. I'd have no career without you guys.

Francessca Wingfield - Thank you for taking my cover idea and cranking it up to one hundred. I'm in love with it!

Thanks to my editor Anna Bloom (you should check out her books too). You make sense of my jumble of words.

Last but not least thank you to my crazy friends. Without you guys I wouldn't have the love, confidence or hilarious stories I need to keep going. Love you!

Lightning Source UK Ltd.
Milton Keynes UK
UKHW020455270221
379370UK00005B/157

9 781916 273467